W9-DHH-858
$ 5.49
18790
376678
AR

This logbook is presented,
with the sailing vessel

Picaroon,

in good faith, to Captain Redbeard.
May you fill these pages with
exploits enacted far from our shores.

Liam O'Sheen

The Honorable Liam O'Sheen

July 17

Time-Ravaged City
Jumbled Jungle
Spangled Beach
Vesper Cliffs
Split Pea Swamp
HEADLANDS
Bandit Range
Candlestick Caverns
The Good Ship Picaroon's Final Mooring
ROSETTA BAY
Red 'n' Black Lands
Geyser Field
Looking Glass River
Redbeard's Den
JAW BONE POINT
Mount Fog Spout
Twin Star Peak
Seaside Pathways
Teetering Peak
The Amazing Crater (Bottomless?)
Lodestone Canyon
"F.I." Lake
Glistering Tunnel Entrance
Quiet Wilds
Exit
THE BIG BEND
Cordillera Central
Red Bean Sound*
Witco Stacks
Unbraved Bush (Marmoond's Pickings)
Quicksand Circles
Roamin' Dunes
Burnt Bridge
TERRA FIRMA
Slate Horn Rock
CAPE ANVIL
Clean Slate Face
THE EXACT AND ONLY MAP OF
FUNDORADO
ISLAND
*I must give credit where it's due. After all, his like did come through in the end.

Redbeard's Discoveries
and His Adventures Too

by Yers Truly,
Captain Redbeard

(with Help from a Lucky Penny)

Delacorte Press

Published by Delacorte Press
an imprint of Random House Children's Books
a division of Random House, Inc.
New York

www.randomhouse.com/kids
Educators and librarians, for a variety of teaching tools,
visit us at www.randomhouse.com/teachers

Library of Congress Cataloging-in-Publication Data
Redbeard, Captain.
Fundorado Island : Redbeard's discoveries (and his adventures too) / by yers truly,
Captain Redbeard ; (with help from a lucky Penny). — 1st ed.
p. cm.
Summary: In his logbook, Captain Redbeard the pirate relates his adventures, including mutiny, ongoing battles with jelly beans, and a mysterious island called Fundorado.
ISBN-13: 978-0-385-73267-3 (hardcover)—ISBN-13: 978-0-385-90284-7 (glb edition)
ISBN-10: 0-385-73267-8 (hardcover)—ISBN-10: 0-385-90284-0 (glb edition)
[1. Pirates—Fiction. 2. Adventure and adventurers—Fiction. 3. Tall tales. 4. Humorous stories.]
PZ7.G339268Fun 2006
[Fic]—dc22
2005036566

The text of this book is set in 14-point Cloister.
Book design by Trish Parcell Watts
Printed in the United States of America
10 9 8 7 6 5 4 3 2 1
First Edition

A NOTE FROM THE PUBLISHER

Dear Reader,

Some time ago, a visitor named Rufus Sherwood came into my office unannounced. He explained that he was a fisherman off the coast of Maine and that he had recently experienced a rather peculiar encounter with a bird unlike any he had ever seen. According to Mr. Sherwood's account, this giant bird swooped down upon his vessel and delivered the logbook of a pirate captain. Mr. Sherwood placed this logbook on my desk while entreating me to consider it for publication. I agreed to read through the material at my earliest convenience, then politely asked him to leave. In addition to the aforementioned material, Mr. Sherwood also left behind the rancid scent of cod, which took me the better part of a month to expunge from my high-back leather chair.

More to the point, what I discovered was precisely what you will soon see for yourself: a masterpiece. And how marvelous it is that this—how shall I say?—free-spirited adventurer is able to have someone with him for the entire breadth of the journey, hanging on to every derring-do detail. You might ask yourself, how does a cold-blooded pirate become an author? Well, my good reader, you will soon find out. . . .

I assure you that we have made every possible effort to accurately reproduce Mr. Redbeard's work. You should also know that I am taking great care in preserving the original scrapbook and have placed it in a secure vault at a secret location.

It has given me great pleasure to discover this story, and it gives me greater pleasure to introduce it to you. I hope you enjoy the journey every bit as much as I did.

Sincerely,
Maxwell Dormpier III
Executive Publisher

Ahoy, Li'l Whisker,

Being a pirate, I've had me share of adventure and heard many a tall tale. But what I'm pulling ye into be more thrilling than any lit keg o' gunpowder I ever had the chance to leap away from. And I must warn ye, me story has more surprises than the Indian Ocean battered by the fists of a typhoon. Go ahead and ask yer grand-pappy to tell ye about the *Odyssey* with its one-eyed Cy-clops, or King Arthur and the Lady of the Lake, or Jack and his beanstalk. But none will be shedding any light on the greatest adventure of 'em all. This here is me very own legend, and the reason it's greater than all the others is very simple: me friend, this story is real. From time to time thar might be parts that are hard to believe, and thar might even be a few turns o' the page where things seem like downright scuttlebutt. But ye have me golden word, every last bit is true. Put on yer sea legs, matey. Stick close to me words—ye wouldn't want to miss a single moment of the journey.

Legends are slippery as eels. Just when ye think ye've a solid grip on 'em, yer shocked at thar knack for slithering out of reach. Now, nobody's too sure when this here legend got its start, but I can tell it to ye straight. This is where the tale caught up with me and tangled me in its wonderful world. And as any swashbuckler will tell ye, an adventure is best when ye don't have it all to yer lonesome self. Lucky for me, I found a very trusty friend along the way.

It's at sea, o' course, that me story starts, in a patch of ocean that sailors call the Bed of Argus. Me crew and I had just fired two warning shots across the bow of a little red cargo ship. Down her deck, me mates lowered the gangplank and rushed aboard. First Mate McGee twirled a length of rope overhead and introduced our identity to the ship's cowering sailors. "We're Cap'n Redbeard's rapscallions! Once again we've caught up with our reputation—the pleasure's yers . . . but the treasure's ours!" His arm swooped forward, then snapped back, lacing a few o' the crew in his lasso.

One of the tangled men proved himself to be quite bright. He cupped his trembling hands to the sides of an unruly mustache and called out to the others, "It's no use, me mates! The *Picaroon*'s blind to all but victory. Thar be no true shame to our surrender."

McGee emptied the buggers' pockets 'n' pouches of the few coins they had to offer. I stepped aboard to make certain any survivors had plenty to warn thar seafaring kin about.

Not a single gold bar, emerald or ruby was uncovered, though the ship did have barrels 'n' crates. We reckoned they just might be holding some treasure, so we nabbed 'em to be on the safe side.

To the tune of clanking swords and whizzing bullets, me and Boggs the Cabin Boy made our way up the cargo ship's mast. I scurried up the pole and turned to look down at the fighting below. Right away I saw the ship's captain sneaking up on one of me most loyal mates, Porthole Pete. In a flash I reached into me coat and pulled out the weapon that helped make me the most feared pirate ever to sail the seven seas (or any sea, for that matter). It weren't no pistol clenched in me fist. . . . It was a paintbrush. Porthole Pete could fend for himself; I was busy making me attack on the ship. When I looked down once more, I saw that, as usual, Boggs was having a hard time reaching the top of the mast. Climbing with a bucket o' paint in each hand was a task he hadn't quite mastered. I was worried that by the time he got up, thar'd be less paint in the pails than thar was on him.

As soon as he caught up with me, I dipped me trusty brush into the black paint and began me infamous assault across the ship's sail. As was me custom, I quickly sketched me own portrait, finishing up with fire red paint for me eyes. Then I went back to the black and put the letters "FI" under me drawing.

Over the years, many a seagoer has misunderstood me sail painting. They thought the letters "FI" were the initials of Ferdinand Igneominious—a name I had escaped long ago. As a lad I could never spell me own name. I had a highwayman scrawl it 'cross the palm o' me hand in case I was put on the spot. No, matey, I wasn't born with the great pirate name Redbeard. It is a name I earned. Of course, I would have liked to be called Blackbeard; it only makes sense. Me beard is black, not red. Alas, I couldn't claim the name Blackbeard, for some two-bit stowaway had already taken it. But I got back at him. We all know which name history will remember best.

Mort

S.O.S. #1

Nom de Plunder

Besides, I'm not the only pirate who changed his name. Calico Jack went by John Rackam, Black Bart was Bartholomew Roberts, that character Bluebeard weren't even a pirate, and Blackbeard himself was Eddie Teach. This isn't all that important, but ye might find it amusing anyhow.

Sometimes the tiniest coins in a treasure are the ones that bring me the most joy. If I find meself with a li'l story or a nugget o' knowledge ye might want to know about, I'll jot it here, off to the side. Just to make sure ye see it coming and don't confuse it with me main story, I'll mark each as a Side-Order Story, or S.O.S. for the short-winded.

I'd cast off me birth name long ago. It honestly had nothing to do with the mystery of "FI." The secret of those two letters goes back to the first sea raid I ever led. In order to let the world know that the oceans now belonged to me, I began the grand tradition of painting a wicked drawing of meself on the mainsail of me poor victims' ship and then scrawling the words "FINDERS KEEPERS!" beneath. It was all in the spirit of black-hearted fun, but I learned on me first attempt that whenever bullets and cannonballs are involved, thar be no time to spare. I was only able to finish the face and the first two letters when a bullet ripped through the sail. With that, me trademark was born. Ever since, me emblem has been met with fear and awe by any sailor who dared to fall under its shadow.

But enough about me—let's get back to me story. Thunderin' blazes, where were we? . . . Oh yes! The li'l red cargo ship! With me sailing signature complete, I stowed the paintbrush deep in me coat pocket and spied young Boggs slide down the mast and zip back to the *Picaroon.* He had already learned the hard way to clear out when I was in the middle of a sea raid.

Far below, Monkey Fist swung on a chain from our railing and landed on the cargo ship's deck. He stood a head and a half over the second tallest man (an awfully long way for his drool to fall). He cornered some unlucky souls up the rigging with his plank and chain. They were all rightfully terrified and no doubt befuddled, too, for Monkey Fist battles in his long johns. That chain, ye see, holds his pants up in times of peace.

I slid down the mast, picked up the biggest crate of all and started back toward me good ship *Picaroon.* As I made me way to the gangplank, I saw our ship's cook, Jonah, trip on a cannonball and tumble over the railing. With some luck he was able to grab hold of the edge of the gangplank as he dangled over the briny deep. Li'l Whisker, let me tell ye, thar was fear in shriveled old Jonah's eyes—but I knew thar might be gold in that thar crate o' mine. I couldn't very well reach down to help

Jonah or I'd risk dropping the crate into the rough waters. So I made me way across the narrow bridge. As I passed to the *Picaroon,* Jonah's fingers happened to find thar way under me boots. After a yelp through his gums, he plunged into the depths. And with him went the secret of Scurvy Rock. What became of him, ye ask? I can't rightly say, but I know one thing for sure . . . the ocean ain't too friendly in those parts. The last thing I saw was his yellow and green polka-dotted bandanna floating atop the waves.

"Oh well," I said through me husky beard, "one less pirate when it comes time to divide the booty." We secured the rest of the barrels 'n' crates, without the help of Jonah, as the cargo ship slowly slipped from sight.

Later that night, the crew gathered round the biggest barrel to see what our hard day's work had brought us. Thar was wonder in the air as First Mate McGee cracked open the wooden top. All eyes were peeled to see whatever mystery treasure lay waiting inside. (All eyes, that is, except for one belonging to Dr. Pauley Wog, who wears a patch cut from the cloth of a general's breeches.) But I'm sorry to say that what McGee revealed was most certainly not treasure. To the contrary, it was more horrifying than anything I could ever imagine. The barrel was crammed to the very top with . . . jelly beans. Red ones. Green ones. Black ones. Every color and flavor known to mankind. I yelled for McGee and the crew to open the other barrels but it was all the same. Jelly beans. Each and every barrel 'n' crate was full of 'em. Now, I know what yer thinking. "Jelly beans don't seem so bad. In fact, they're kind of tasty." Well, me friend, I've got me reasons for having such a keen hatred of those blasted candies. Ye see, jelly beans don't look so good and they don't smell so good and they sure as day don't taste so good if ye've had all yer front teeth rotted off by the li'l pills o' sugar. True, I gobbled 'em down as a wee lad, and maybe too many, because they left me toothless! Aye, everyone used to poke fun at me and me bare gums.

But all that joking came to an end one dark day when I met up with Black Finn, the most frightening shark in Flotsam Bay. We tussled a bit and he escaped—but not with his teeth. From that day on, no one dared to make fun of me anymore, for I had robbed the ocean's most dangerous animal of its only weapon. I made a visit to Shellfish Davey's cousin, a dentist by hobby alone. He fixed the pointy devils into the pits o' me gums. (One of the many bonuses of having a few shark teeth is that I can whittle the most handsome likenesses out o' corncobs.)

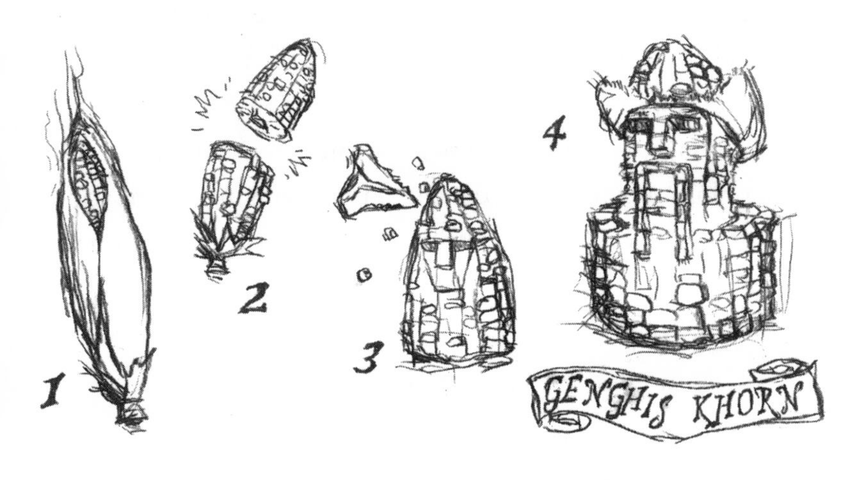

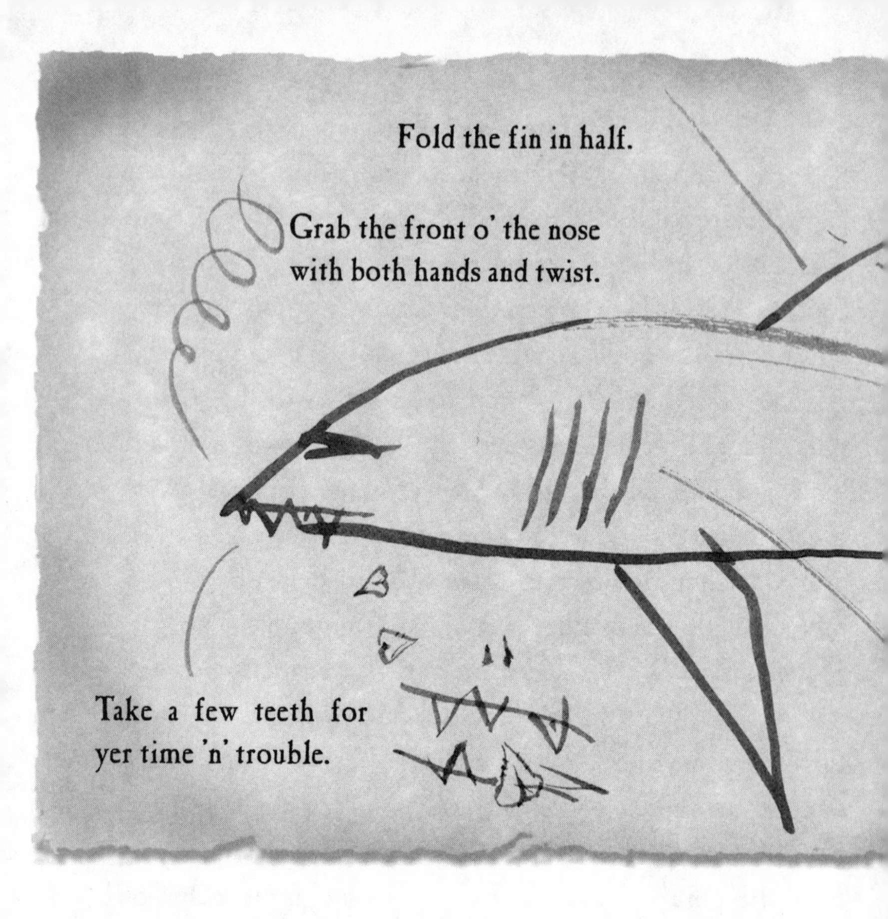

No, me friend, I didn't much like the sight of those sorry jelly beans. Opening up the barrels took me right back to those toothless times, and I suddenly became quite angry indeed. I ordered me crew to throw all the barrels overboard. Then I stormed down to me cabin hoping to catch some decent shuteye and put the horrible evening behind me. I settled into me nighttime routine.

I worked me scuffed boots off me aching feet and removed me tricorn hat. I reached up into the secret

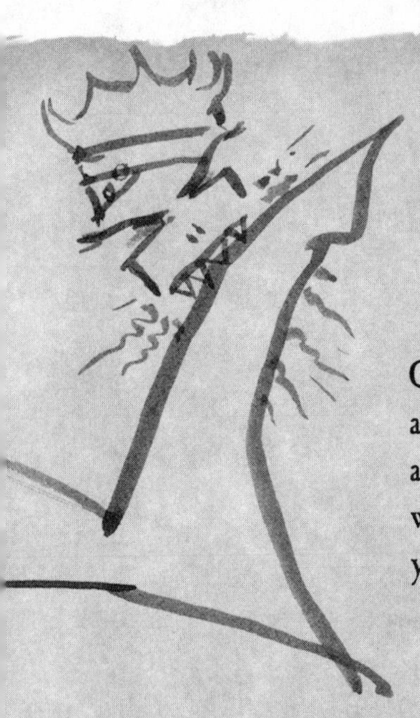

S.O.S. #2

Fishticuffs

Grip the tail with both yer fists and don't be afraid o' swingin' to and fro. He can't find ye when yer way back thar. And while yer at it, ye can give his tail a nibble or two.

Give the ole gills a tickle. Thar's no spot more tickly.

pouch sewn into the lining and pulled out the golden key to me personal treasure. Now, don't be confusing me own personal treasure with the booty that me band o' rogues loots from other ships. The riches in this chest are mine. And they ain't to be shared! (Being greedy is easy when ye've got really good stuff.) Deep inside me trunk is something ye won't be finding in any other. Me treasure chest is extra special. In fact, it's king-sized. King-sized enough to hold a baby hippo.

S.O.S. #3

A Trunk Fit for a Hippo

Thar we were, in the Indian Ocean off the coast o' Zanzibar. Legends in the region claimed that beyond the Rufiji River, past a shroud of curling thorns and at the bottom of a bat-lined cave, a nest of spitting cobras writhed in front of a black widow's web, which was spun across a passageway that led to a chamber where thousands of scorpions danced along the edge of a foaming pool of poison. But the natives' stories didn't stop thar. For at the bottom of that dangerous pool a ruby cut in the shape of an apple sat for the taking. I had to add the ruby to me collection o' riches.

Up the river we ventured, our backs boiling beneath the sun's stinging blaze. We discovered many caves, but even with the help of our lanterns we were unable to locate the ruby. We must have explored twenty caves and they all revealed the same thing: nothing! Over the bank, Googler pointed out a modest-sized opening. Thar weren't no sharp thorns guarding it. And it didn't look particularly scary. Maybe the legend alone was enough to keep greedy treasure hunters at bay.

We breezed into the tunnel and were met with no dangers—not a bat to be found. No cobras or scorpions. The only creepy crawling thing that stood in our way was a slow-leaking stinkbug. I reached down and nabbed the brilliant apple. "Har-har, me hearties, an easy prize she is. An easy prize indeed." Along the rock walls the crew's cheers echoed and we all filed out with our hands clamped around our noses.

From the dark I returned to the blistering glare of the

sunlight. The rotten stench of the stinkbug grew worse, forcing the band of men from the cave's slim mouth. They pushed and shoved, racing for fresh air.

On the narrow ledge outside the entrance, we all stumbled, blinded by the scorching summer sky. A pirate (and to this day I still don't know who) bumped me from behind, making me drop the giant ruby off the ledge. Still blinded, I was unable to see the apple fall but I did hear it splat in the mud on the riverbank below. Me eyes adjusted to the sun in time to see the ruby sparkling in the dark muck. Coming upon me treasure was a hungry baby hippo. Down its jaw went to scoop up the deliciously shaped ruby, and down the steep slope me men slid to capture it. The hippo, while just a youngun, was as strong as eight men (ten wrestled it to the ground, but Maximilian and Measles Gilroy didn't really help that much).

The ruby apple was gobbled up by the animal, so we had to wait until nature returned it to us. For lack of a proper hippo cage, I decided to use me treasure trunk as a holding pen.

Down below, I settled for bed, knowing that in the morning I would have me ruby. I tried to get to sleep but the excitement was too much. I couldn't wait. Into the lock I slipped the key, hoping to find the ruby. As the trunk clicked open, the hippo burst out, bucking wildly about me cabin. Back and forth it ran. I lunged for it. Even with me husky force, I couldn't hold it. Baby hippos are strong. It took ten men to capture it but only one to let it go. Over the treasure chest it leapt, crashing right through the portholes and into the sea below. Ever since, I've never had a ruby apple. Ruby rings and scepters, sure. But nary another stone cut in the shape of delicious fruit.

First I lifted the top and revealed the mountain o' twinklin' coins. In heaping handfuls I gathered up the golden doubloons and threw 'em into me old sugar barrel, and as for what was left I tossed it into me hat. With the chest cleared out, I reached to the bottom and swung open a trapdoor, revealing me true treasure. Thar it was. Me pride and glory. In me early days, as a young cabin boy, I was eager to gain the respect of the whole crew. But no matter what I did, they'd shrug it off. Soon I realized I'd have to do something impossible. . . .

At that time, we were docked at Dunderhead, a land ruled by the great King Cornelius. One day it hit me like a cannon blast: what could be more impossible than swiping the crown right off a king's head?

As the rest of the crew slept slung in their hammocks, I snuck out for me secret mission. Swifter than the sirocco, I ran all the way from the wharf to the king's castle, and in barely a breath I was over the wall and under the gun. Through spots of moonglow I patiently braved me way across the forecourt. A wolfhound snored, halfway out of his li'l wooden home. How lucky was I to find a watchdog able to sleep soundly amidst the clamor of duty's call? A hop had me on top of the animal's house (the roof whined a bit beneath me boots) and a step had me at the foot of a great thorned lattice, stretching straight up the towering face of the castle.

I scaled the prickly trellis and, being a skinny cabin boy, I was able to slip through the window bars and leap into the sleeping king's chamber. The fool even guarded the sacred crown in his sleep! It was resting atop his head! I waited for him to roll over, and when he did, I seized the golden opportunity by snatching the crown and bolting for the window. Me body wriggled past the iron poles, but me arm, with crown in tow, trailed behind. I tugged at the treasure, hoping to pop it free. It wouldn't budge. Against the bars I leaned, and me heart pumped in couplets as I jerked the crown through with a fitful force. The bold move worked! But the tragedy of it was that the crown slipped from me hand and twirled toward the sleeping guard dog below. The noisy shot cut into the mongrel's nap and held him square in the midnight shadow of the falling crown.

Li'l Whisker, it was a direct hit! I take a lot of pride in clean marksmanship (even if it comes by accident). The crown sank over the dog's head as a ring might bejewel some lovely lady's finger.

King Cornelius began to stir from the racket, so down the trellis I ripped, nearly quicker than a fall would have landed me. It must have been a sight, me rushing along the castle lawn with the hound's crowned head just pinches away from me flailing legs. And no matter how hard he tried, he couldn't move his mouth with the crown ringing his head. Thar must've been a hundred angry fangs in his jaws and they were all useless. That poor dog just couldn't get a taste. . . . How brilliant that the treasure could serve as such blooming good protection from the beast.

When I climbed to the top o' the wall, I reached back as the hound sprang up, trying to catch me. I hooked me legs around a torch sticking from the stones, and when the animal leapt again, I latched on to the crown with the stubborn grip of a barnacle. The dog twisted in the air, its weight almost splitting me in two. Me fingers purpled under the pressure before a pop sent the hound tumbling to the ground. His furious growling tore the night into tatters, waking the village, but of course I was gone before any of that mattered. Ever since, I've had me very own crown.

Needless to say, the royal heist granted me immediate promotion to full-fledged pirate.

Never did I forget that the crown led to me captainhood. So every night I would place it upon me head and look down through me cabin window at the white-capped waves, pretending they were me subjects. I'd wish me

kingdom a good night's sleep and then return the crown to its secret hiding spot.

Ye might count them jumping sheep to get to sleep, but I find comfort in counting me gold coins. Tossing the doubloons back into the chest could always lull me into dreamland. Once the crown and coins were safely stowed, I hopped on top of me treasure chest and snuggled up under me checkered quilt. It may sound a wee bit uncomfortable, but let's see ye try to get a sound sleep with unguarded treasure in yer cabin. Thar be only one problem with the cozy setup: me legs hung over the ledge of the trunk. So I kept them propped up in me giant hammock. I reached beyond the covers for the sleepwalking straps bolted to the sides of me trunk. To be sure, it's not the most usual way to get yer shuteye. I'll take dozing under the buckle over waking up in some of those embarrassing spots me sleepwalking has run me into. Li'l Whisker, if I don't lock meself down, I will start to wander.

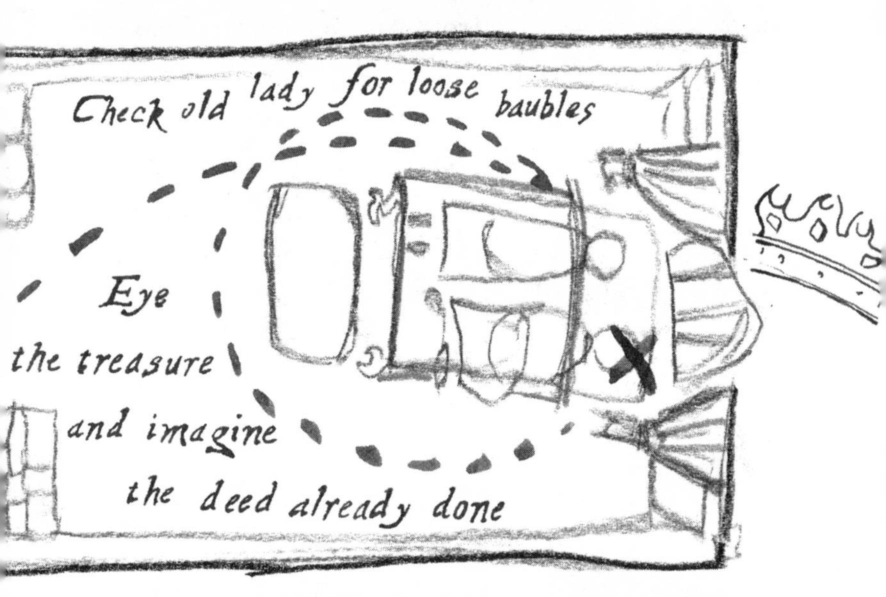

Before me eyes could find the dreams the night had in store, a slight knock-knock came from me door. (A quick nautical lesson: ships are loud, restless things, always creaking and groaning. If yer gonna knock, give it some muscle!) Me weak-armed visitor turned out to be Boggs the Cabin Boy. His voice, swaddled in nervousness, made scarcely a mumble through the door. "Cap'n Redbeard, sir. I beg yer pardon for the interruption."

From atop me treasure I responded, "I'll pardon the interruption if ye could interrupt a li'l louder. I can hardly hear ye!"

His words raised a few notches. "Might I have permission to enter, then?"

"Well, I can't rightly see the need now, Boggs—I can understand ye just dandy. And besides, me light's already out." I pressed the boy on the point of the intrusion. "Me last command was for the entire crew to dump those miserable candies down to the blackest pit o' Davey Jones's locker. I know ye 'n' the rest o' the no-good noddies up top couldn't possibly have tossed every barrel overboard yet. So I'm curious—what is it ye want?"

It sounded as if he pushed his face just above the doorknob. When he spoke, he was using the keyhole as a mouthpiece. "It's the jelly beans, sir. First Mate McGee has an idea about 'em. . . ."

I shot right back with me answer. "I already gave McGee an idea 'bout them beans. He's supposed to get rid of 'em. Right now!"

"That's just it, Cap'n. He thinks it a good idea to save 'em. Said somethin' 'bout the Duke of Dunkirk. This gent has a powerful sweet tooth. We could trade 'em beans. Thar like barrels full o' gold." The scrod's voice bobbed with delight. He really thought First Mate McGee was on to something.

"May I ask ye a question, dear Boggs?"

"O' course, sir."

"Who is the captain of the *Picaroon*?"

"Ye are, Cap'n Redbeard, sir."

"Then answer me this. How'd ye like me to jettison those candy crates all by me lonesome? And for any swab who didn't help, meanin' every last one of ye lazy gherkins, I'll cast ye off into the sea as well . . . sink or swim."

Boggs swept out his words in a hurry. "Understood, sir. Me hands are needed up top. I don't need anyone drawin' me up to be a loafer. Good night to ye, Cap'n." And he scurried off.

"McGee. Again with his thoughts and opinions," I muttered to meself. "He likes his seas rough, does he?" The men were on the main deck, right over me cabin. With enough wind in me sails, I could get his attention.

"McGee, put yer ear to the floorboards!" I threw me voice up above. "Yer not in control here. I am! Thar isn't a shift of the rudder that I don't know about. I am the captain, thar ain't nothin' more mighty. Do ye hear me up thar?"

"Aye."

Again I railed up to the crossbeams. "And if ye don't like sailin' with the fiercest crew that ever was, ye can take a dip in the drink 'n' hope a schooner comes by to scoop ye out. Do I make meself clear?"

His voice dropped flatly from overhead. "Aye."

Aye. What music to me ears. With the knowledge that I was in agreement with me crew, I excused me mind to the glories of slumber.

The night, she passed quickly. I was awakened by the sun streaming through me cabin window. On most mornings, it would be an unwelcome sight, for a pirate loves his slumber. But on that thar morning, I couldn't wait to start the day with the cursed jelly beans behind me.

S.O.S. #4

Life on the High ZZZ's

Boggs the Cabin Boy slept right through chore time aboard the *Picaroon*. Me and the crew tried to make his life as easy as possible. Early on in his days, as an extra hand on ship, Boggs climbed into the portside cannon, taking orders from First Mate McGee to give it a solid scrubbing. Completely unaware of the unauthorized order, I asked Monkey Fist to fire some practice rounds at a rickety dock jutting out from a nearby shore. He lit the wick and the heavy gun roared, launching dear young Boggs over the cresting swells. Thankfully, Monkey Fist's aim was no better than a blindfolded bat's. Boggs missed the wooden pier and landed instead in a small boat tied to a post. The speed that the li'l cabin boy reached sent the boat skimming along the water, snapping the mooring rope as I'd pluck a gray whisker from me beard. The boat finally stopped upon the beach, where it sat halfway under the sand. Monkey Fist held his breath, waiting to see if Boggs would be all right. When we saw the thin, freckled arm rise out of the boat, we knew he would be fine. Upon his safe return to the ship, Monkey Fist vowed to take care of all Boggs's chores. The pirate felt so bad he even offered to let the youngster fire him from the cannon. Boggs accepted, too, the only problem being Monkey Fist was so heaped with muscles, he could scarcely fit his arm down the cannon shoot.

Turned out I had to sit and wait in me cabin a spell. Boggs the Cabin Boy was late with me apple cider. As sure as the sea's salty, that cider was always thar waitin' for me when I woke. The young pirate would set me hot drink on me sugar barrel and wake me with a song. His voice cracked and his notes went sour, but still, it was always nice to wake up to a tune. Of course, I could have gone for the cider meself, what with the galley being right below me cabin. But I knew it wouldn't be fair to Boggs, seeing how his onliest duty on board was getting me that drink.

And so I waited . . . and waited. Boggs the Cabin Boy never showed. I unbuckled me sleepwalking straps, put on me hat and headed up to the main deck to give him a real what-for.

As I rushed through the hall at full sail, I was met with an ill feeling. Did me memory serve me correct? Wasn't Monkey Fist on swabbing detail? Aye! He was! Just like Boggs the Cabin Boy, he was nowhere to be seen. Li'l Whisker, that was when I knew something was fishy. On me tiptoes, I crept up the narrow stairs. Every step squeaked squeaky as the squeakiest mouse. (Maybe even squeakier.)

As I flung the heavy door open, this is what me eyes fell upon. 'Twas attached high on the mast, a fork poked through it so the wind couldn't have at it. (Better ye read it first. Then I'll tell ye how it struck me.)

To Our Dear Captain Redbeard,

I, McGee, being first mate of the Picaroon, have worked with ye the longest. That means I also have the biggest dislike for ye. At a vote of 10 to 1, I was voted purtiest penmanship, so I have the honor of saying . . . WE LEFT YE!!! Our reasons are as follows:

1. *Ye takes more than yer fair share of the treasure.*
2. *Ye takes more than yer fair share of the rations.*
3. *Because of number two, yer breath's always stinky.*
4. *Relating to number three, ye always yell in our faces.*
5. *When thinking about number one, ye should have enough gold to buy a clean shirt.*
6. *Measles Gilroy said he had a good one but he forgot what it was.*
7. *That tattoo ye have, the mermaid—it ain't fit for a ne'er-do-well like ye. What about something more piratey, like a skull 'n' crossbones. . . . That's what every other member o' the crew has.*
8. *Plain and simple, yer just plain mean and simple—even for a pirate.*

The long and short of it is Maximilian saw what you did to Jonah and spread word of the terrible deed on to the whole crew. A captain's supposed to watch over his men—not watch them fall out from under him! Ye've sunk lower than a pirate should go. I would make a better captain than ye and that's why the whole crew voted 10 to 1 to make me their new captain. Captain McGee. Me first order as captain is to have the crew load the escape dinghy with these items:

1. *All the food.*
2. *All the weapons.*

3. Gold, red rubies, and green emeralds from our most recent raids.
4. Yer favorite scope. (If ye miss it, ye can always stare at the cover of yer logbook.)
5. Mort left his drawing pad behind as a sort of offering (so that ye may remember the better times).

On second thought, we've taken so much it would be easier to tell ye what we have left behind:

1. One cannonball.
2. One map.
3. Yer beloved treasure chest (we couldn't lift ye without waking ye. Besides, it's huge! We don't even know how you got it through your cabin door. Maximilian said the ship was certainly built around it).
4. 212,025 jelly beans—at last count!!! (Did ye say throw 'em overboard? We thought ye said put 'em belowdecks. Sorry. We know how much ye love the candies so we stowed 'em in the galley, right next to yer cabin. We left one barrel up above so ye could have the honor of moving it yerself.)

In conclusion, yer nothing without yer crew. And come to think of it, we're better off without ye because ye make us:

1. miserable.
2. angry.
3. sometimes both miserable and angry at the same time.

Also in conclusion, nobody thinks ye will make it. Googler thinks Black Finn is sure to get his teeth back in no time and Maximilian thinks that without him manning the wheel ye will most certainly steer right into a hurricane.

One last conclusion. When we were packing our things to leave from the Picaroon, Jimmy couldn't find his accordion. If ye find it, leave it alone. His grandpa gave it to him. DO NOT TOUCH IT! IT'S HIS!

—Yer Former Crew
First Mate McGee
Mort
Lt. Googler
Jimmy O'Boyle
Dr. Pauley Wog
Billy Bilgewater
Monkey Fist
Porthole Pete
Boggs the Cabin Boy
Measles Gilroy
Maximilian, Tiger of Trinidad
X________________
(This is where Jonah would have signed, ye filthy animal!)

What an embarrassing lot! Can ye believe they actually thought they would make it without me? Captain McGee, *ha!* No crew would respect a short and scrawny captain. Thar ain't no spine in his back and his baby teeth were too pigeon-livered to fall out into such a cruel world. He couldn't captain a toy boat in a bubble bath, let alone a rowboat through the Bed of Argus. Li'l Whisker, I've been sailing the deep blue for nearly three score years. It's happened to me before. A group of landlubbers lacking what it takes to be true pirates. They might last a couple of raids, but they'll never measure up to me strict standards. I run a tight ship, ye see; it's no pleasure cruise.

'Tweren't no disaster setting out on me own that morning. I could run the ship just fine by me lonesome till I picked up another crew. I heard thar was a tiny island off

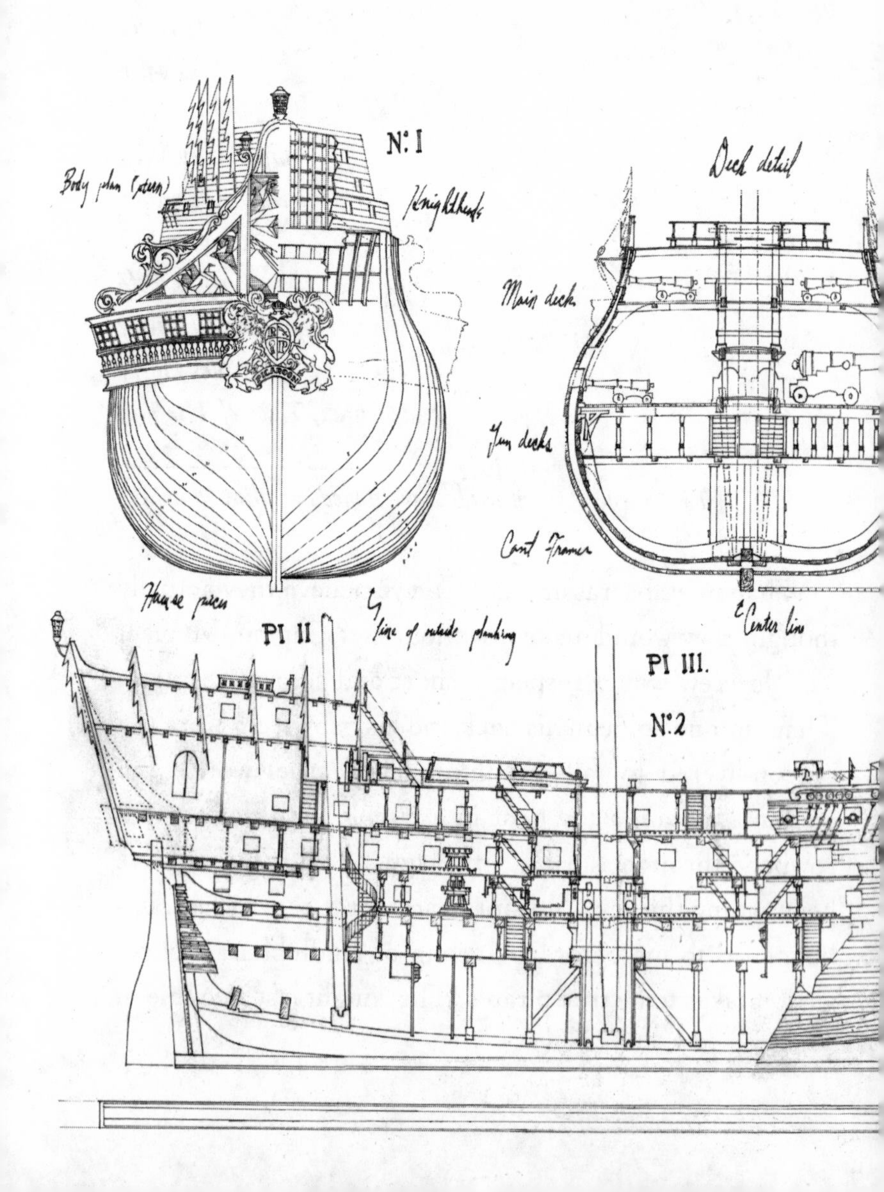

of Madagascar where a captain's sure to find some worthyhelp. So I headed south. I began by setting the sails (one of 'em was ripped, so I sewed it right up). Next, I tightened the rigging and manned the wheel. Being a real pirate, I know that a tidy ship is a mighty ship, so I swabbed the deck and took the knots out of the anchor line. All the while, between me tasks, I would climb up to the crow's nest to keep watch.

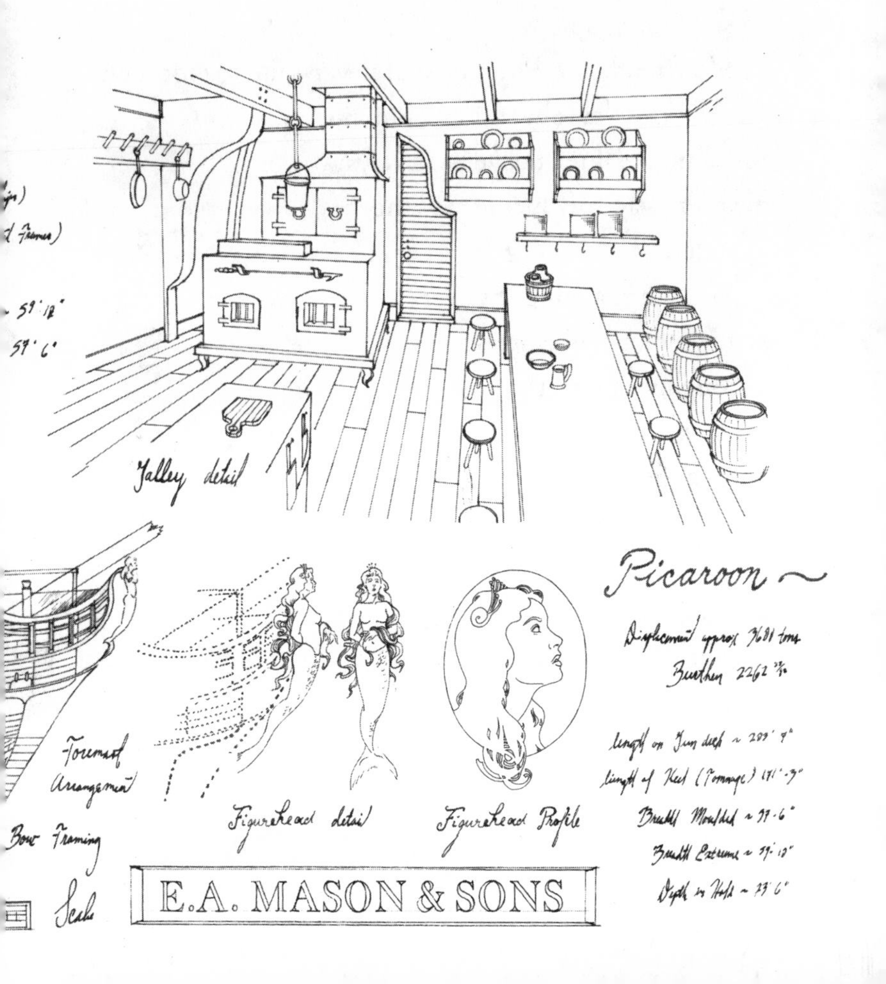

Oh, the merry moment that greeted me up above the freshly scrubbed deck. Turns out the decision to abandon the *Picaroon* wasn't unanimous. I weren't alone after all, for ole Wellington stayed behind. Thar he was, sleeping like a baby in the crow's nest. His long yellow bill quivered under his wings as he quietly squawked in his li'l birdy dreams. Wellington the Pelican is just behind yers truly in his number o' years on the *Picaroon.* He keeps to himself, far from the reach of the hustle below. I'd gone months without seeing or thinking o' the fella. It was nice to see him again.

Me friend, the *Picaroon* had never sailed smoother. Clear skies lay ahead . . . but not for long. Blue heavens always have a way of luring in the thunder.

Manning a ship by yerself, ye can build up quite a loneliness in the ole tummy. Knowing the crew had left me with nary a spoonful of Jonah's tasty salmagundi or a stale ship biscuit, I was sure them jelly bean barrels were calling me name.

S.O.S. #5

Deep-Sea Salamagundi

Jonah the sea cook was a wizard of the crock. He could concoct a mouthwatering dish from a mound of limp vegetables and stinky meat. And it was a good thing too, because that's all he had to work with on board the *Picaroon*. He prepared his signature meal, "Deep-Sea Salmagundi," hidden away in the galley, so any ingredients and cooking methods were a complete mystery to me. Even still, I spent countless dinners slurping the stuff down, so I think I can rightly figure out how he did it.

DEEP-SEA SALMAGUNDI

(Makes enough for a hungry crew with a li'l left over for Wellington the Pelican)

10 slightly shriveled potatoes, peeled and stabbed
8 carrots all hacked to pieces
6 fish, preferably not a poisonous variety
1 purple thing (I think it was an onion.)
Enough spices to cover the taste

Place all ingredients in a large pot, but before ye put the stuff in, make sure some boiling water is already thar. Stir it when ye feel like it. If yer bored, ye can mash it up with a masher or ye can wait and mash it with yer teeth when ye chew it. When it really starts bubbling it's done cooking. Scoop out and serve. If ye don't like it, toss it overboard for a quick and easy shark repellent.

No matter how loud me stomach growled, I wouldn't even turn and look at 'em. I kept me eyes on the sea. The winds picked up and the late afternoon slowly became evening. Every minute crawled by. All I was thinking about was getting me hands on some food. I'm sure if ye were in me boots, ye'd've been fishing by then. But of course, yer no-good crew wouldn't have taken yer fishing poles and left ye with nothing but a hungry belly. It bristled me beard having to watch all them marlin jumping in and out of the waves just ahead of me ship. They were no good to me without a fishing pole. I could have gathered some rope and tried me hand at hauling 'em in with a slick lasso, but seeing as the crew hadn't left enough spare rope to tie up me boots, I couldn't rightly give it a whirl. I needed to make a fishing pole.

I dashed down to me cabin and grabbed me emergency pirate kit. I knew it'd be one of the only things the crew hadn't gotten thar hands on, seeing how it was hidden safe and sound behind me empty sugar barrel.

On deck, I opened up the dusty wood box and brought out me supplies. One eye patch, in case I lost me eye. One peg leg, in case I lost me leg. One giant hook, in case I lost me hand. And one backup Jolly Roger. Ye can always tell the skilled buccaneer from the clumsy swab. Here be an example: the skilled buccaneer will return with his treasure and escape a battle unharmed, but the clumsy swab will return without his treasure, his hand or his foot. Matey, I've got both hands, both feet, and both eyes—spot-on vision, as a matter of fact. That should be more than enough to let ye judge what kind o' pirate I am. I was only keeping the emergency kit because I was preparing for the worst. A good pirate always expects the unexpected.

I took the Jolly Roger in me hands and tore it into five long strips. After tying 'em end to end and connecting the eye patch, I had me very own homemade rope. Then I secured one end to the peg leg and the other to the big hook. Before ye could say "Polly wanna cracker," I had meself an honest-to-goodness fishing pole. For bait I reached down into the jelly bean barrel. Touching just one of the blasted beans shivered me timbers, but I mustered enough courage to bring it out and pop it onto the end of the hook. For all I hate the candies, that little black jelly bean looked mighty funny on the end of that big silver hook.

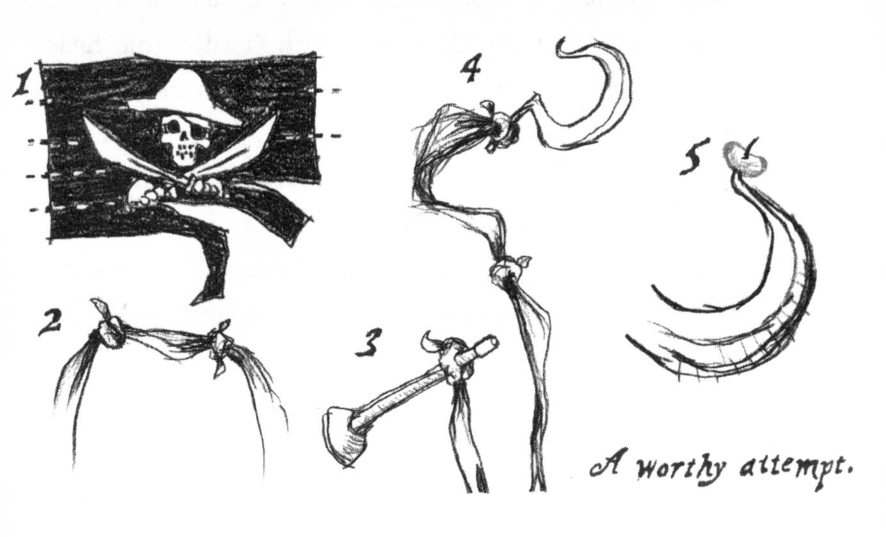

I hoped the little fishies liked jelly beans more than I did. I reared the peg leg pole back and cast the line toward the sun. By the great horn spoon, I didn't even have me fisherman's footing when the line was suddenly ripped from me hands! I reached after it but it was gone. The bean, the hook, the pole—everything vanished into the sea. Me last hope had disappeared.

It was just me and the jelly beans.

Li'l Whisker, please don't think I went against me word. I could've held out forever and a fortnight, but me stomach's willpower was much less admirable. With deep regret, I again reached down into the sinister barrel, not to bait a hook but to fill me belly. I brought out a handful, but it was too much. I tossed them all back and kept only one. The remaining bean was red, a truly fitting color.

Thinking even one bean to be too many, I cut it in two with me sword and chose the smaller half for me first bite. With me eyes closed, I imagined I was feasting on the hot and fresh bread of me youth. I tilted me head back and dropped half of the red jelly bean into me mouth. Believe it or not, the candy had a hint of pumpernickel. Slowly, I ate the other half of the bean and the taste grew even stronger. Still with the taste of the bread on me mind, I placed a second jelly bean on me tongue. Call me crazy as a six-armed sea star, but that jelly bean didn't just taste like pumpernickel, it *was* pumpernickel! Next thing I knew, half the barrel was empty. I was stuffed. At the end of me meal, I licked me fingers and was shocked to find that they tasted like orange, black licorice and cherry. Thar weren't a trace of pumpernickel. It wasn't too long before me belly was gurgling. I stumbled about the deck, rubbing me poor, aching gut. From up top in the crow's nest, the curious Wellington tilted his head to study the sad sight I must've been. In a snap me knees gave out and I slumped against the barrel.

I was too tired and weak to hobble to me cabin and fall asleep safely under me sleepwalking straps. Unwisely, I decided to call it a night and catch forty winks under the stars. A heavy fog folded in as me bleary eyes slowly drew shut.

Matey, the dream I had that night on the deck of the *Picaroon* set the course for an entirely new journey. As ye probably guessed, me dream was about those blasted candies. I couldn't get them out of me head—even in slumber!

The dream started off quickly with me snoring against the old barrel. Then I heard a voice calling me name. Startled, I opened me eyes to see the candy barrel jerking back and forth. As if blasting from a cannon, a huge yellow and green speckled jelly bean shot out of the barrel and landed in the middle of the deck. It was a jelly bean beast! He was as big as a portly cabin boy. His eyes were dark and evil, his teeth were tangled and sharp, and each time he growled, his breath spit forth a candy-scented blast. Right thar, in the middle of me dream, I screamed at the sight of the creature.

Just as I rose to me feet, two more vile candy beasts

emerged from the barrel. One was youthful. When he growled, his voice cracked and went sour. The other was short and scrawny. They flanked the green and yellow speckled monster. All three of 'em stood thar staring at me like an angry crew. I feared for me life.

In an instant, they hopped toward me. I turned, scrambled across the deck and headed down to me cabin with the three candy creatures in me tracks. Panicked, I slammed the door with them one step behind. As soon as I slid under me hammock for safety, they were already busy pounding away at the door. I knew they had me trapped and it was only a matter of time. Whatever those monsters wanted from me, they were about to get it. The hinges snapped and the door burst open. They hopped into the middle of me cabin and stood thar growling and staring me down. Without warning, the green and yellow speckled one ordered me to stand. Using the hammock to steady meself, I hoisted meself up. The huge beast in the middle hopped one more step forward and thrust a scroll into me palm. With quivering hands I unrolled the yellow paper. It was a contract. And if memory serves, it read as follows:

I, Captain Redbeard, do hereby and solemnly swear that I do, always have, always will, currently still, and right now love jelly beans.

I promise.

X________________

Captain Redbeard

I looked up in horror to see the short and scrawny bean holding a pen. The youthful monster with the cracking voice ordered me to sign. I kept telling meself it was a nightmare, but it seemed so real. I was terrified at the thought of taking such a vulgar oath. Immediately I turned me back on the monsters and ripped the yellowed paper into as many pieces as I could.

It was thar that me dream ended. As I opened me eyes, me hands were still tearing apart the contract. I stopped meself as soon as I could, for I realized thar weren't no contract in me hands. It's a solemn thing to tell, but in that moment I saw I had ripped up me only map. The jelly beans were to blame. They had given me a nightmare so bloodcurdling I had acted it out. Like the biggest chicken of the sea, I had run across the deck in me sleep, gone down to me cabin, grabbed me only map and torn it to smithereens. Now that I was fully awake, I knew thar were no jelly bean creatures, they weren't attacking me and, worst of all, thar weren't no contract.

Matey, I'd be lying if I told ye the dream didn't leave me a bit rattled. Right away I ran up to the main deck to make sure everything was shipshape. The good news is that I didn't see any jelly bean beasts. The bad news is that I couldn't have seen 'em even if they'd been thar! The moment I stepped out onto the deck, I saw that the *Picaroon* was crow's-nest deep in a heavy fog. Of course, I'd been in heavy fogs before, but this was by far the worst I'd ever seen. It was as if the ship had fallen into a steaming pot o' clam chowder. Right away, I knew I was in for a long day.

Still without any rations on board, I knew I needed the jelly beans. So I stumbled me way through the murkiness, over to the bean barrel on the other side of the deck. Despite me nightmare, I reached down and grabbed a few handfuls of the candies. In fact, I stuffed me pockets with enough of the beans to get me through the day. Me paintbrush rested at the bottom of me pocket, buried in the disgusting treats. Considering the fog, it was useless for me to try to steer the ship. So I decided to give it a while and see if the murk wouldn't melt away.

It weren't easy, but eventually I walked me way through the chowder to the center of the deck and sat up against the mast. I can't rightly say how long I was waiting. Seeing how the sun was hiding behind the haze, I wasn't sure how much time had passed. Finally, I gave up waiting for the sky to clear. Me only hope was steering me way through the thick patch.

Thar weren't much chance o' getting me new first mate, Wellington, to man the helm, so I stood up and grabbed the wheel meself. No direction seemed better than the others, so I settled on a hard starboard. (Meaning I turned right.)

I knew I had covered a fair distance, but still it seemed as if the *Picaroon* hadn't moved an inch. I had no idea what time it was and I had no way of figuring it out, so I decided to make it me own personal favorite time o' day:

S.O.S. #6

Polly Wanna Chatter

Sailors are a curious lot, to be sure. A more hardworking bunch you'll never meet. But when it comes to thar brains, too much space is taken up by seafaring information, like the 210 different kinds of knots ye can use to secure a jib sail. Thar noggins just can't fit all the stuff regular folks learn in school. So in a touching effort to sound smart, pirates and others on the high seas use code words for common things to bedevil the landlubbers. Here be some examples:

starboard = right
port = left
fore = front
aft = back

To tell ye the truth, Li'l Whisker, I might use a lot of words that are strange and unfamiliar. To help ye on yer way through the story, I'll be listing the words with thar proper definitions in the back of me book for ease of reading. It's the least I can do. Here be one to get ye started: "onomatopoeia."

lunch! Lunchtime is best when you spend it with something other than lousy beans. Li'l Whisker, I'm sure wherever ye are on land, ye can sink yer teeth into some nice peanut butter and jelly sandwich. I don't need to remind ye; ye already know what I had for lunch. After finishing me measly meal, I heard the sails rippling. The winds were picking up. At first they filled me with hope, as I thought they would clear the skies of the dense fog. It sounds a bit odd, but the gusts were actually blowing more fog onto the already overflowing deck. A fear came into me heart as I imagined another ship unwittingly cutting through the clouds straight into the *Picaroon.* I panicked. I ran through the white void to the bow. In an effort to warn nearing crews of me presence, I hollered at the sea. "Avast thar, me ship's caught in a fog," I shouted off into the distance every now and again. When me fears had been calmed, I turned around to find me way back belowdecks. It was then that the voice of a sweet miss sliced through the chowder.

"Ship coming in due east!"

I nearly jumped out o' me boots. "Where are ye? I can't see ye?"

"I can see you." The voice sounded closer yet.

I tried to locate the boat in the fog but I didn't have much luck. So I yelled again, "Drop anchor, ye swab!"

"Who are you calling a swab, Redbeard?"

"What the blazes? Who are ye? How do ye know me name?" I figured she might have heard of me reputation as a fierce pirate. "Ah, was it me triumph at the Salt Flats ye heard about? Or was it when I sank Admiral Gulliver's galleon? Wait, it wasn't Scurvy Rock, was it? Nobody knows about Scurvy Rock!"

"I haven't gotten any word of your skills as a pirate, but I have heard plenty about your failures as a captain."

Right away me beard began to bristle. "Failures? I was at the top o' me class at the Pirate Academy, I was captain before I was even old enough to shave and, as if ye haven't heard, I swiped King Cornelius's crown right off his head."

"But tell me, Redbeard, if you're such a good captain, where's your crew?"

"Wait, how'd ye know me crew be missin'?" I stood thar waiting for the voice to answer me, but thar was only a long silence. I called out to the young miss, but she didn't answer. Could it be that staying all alone on the *Picaroon* for too long had me hearing unnatural things? I couldn't rightly be sure. Still, she had me worried. I had to bring lanterns on deck to warn any closely passing ships of me whereabouts.

I went belowdecks and snatched up the two lanterns the crew had left on the walls. I brought them up and held one in each of me hands as I leaned over the edge of the railing and called out to the soft voice once more. While I waited for a reply, I hung one of the lanterns at the stern and drew me sword for good measure. Then I ran to the front of the deck, leaned over and secured the other lamp in the hand of the mermaid figurehead. The soft glow lit up her wooden face. Even with the dim light of the lamps I couldn't make out where the voice had been coming from. Out of the mist a forward breeze reached out and tipped the hat off me head. In a hurry, I grabbed for it and was able to catch it in time. But it came at a cost. In me haste I dropped me sword into the deep waters and, more importantly, the key to me precious treasure tumbled out and splashed below. Me eyes followed the sound—they found nothing through the fog. I could scarcely see the lovely carved face right in front of me. To be sure, me key was a-plummeting straight for Davey Jones's locker.

I stood thar in the fog waiting for a spell with me arms draped over the railing. I stared into the water, longing after the key, for that was all I could do. Soon the cold creeped under me jacket. Me teeth began to chatter a bit and me husky forearms sprouted goose bumps, so I decided it was bedtime.

I went down below and settled into me nighttime routine. Only without the key, thar weren't no nighttime routine. Li'l Whisker, ye have no idea how sorry I felt for me crown locked away all alone in that dark treasure chest. A treasure just isn't a treasure if thar be no one to appreciate it. The trunk might just as well have been full o' rotten sardines.

Because it was a terribly cold night, I knew I'd be needing an extra blanket. So I made me way over to the old crew's chambers. In the dark room I spied a couple o' blankets piled up in the corner. I reached down to grab one and felt something strange underneath. When I pulled away both blankets, thar on the floor I saw Jimmy's old accordion slumped up against the wall. Remembering how Jimmy's sweet tunes always lifted the spirits of the crew, I sat down to see if any of the melodies could cheer me up. I couldn't rightly touch the instrument with me bare hands, since that no-good McGee had told me not to, so I picked it up with a blanket over me fingers. Only when I squeezed the accordion, it weren't the same. A numbing hum and a hiccup rolled out. No fooling, Li'l Whisker, an honest-to-goodness hiccup. I guess with no music lessons a hiccup was the best I could muster. The earsplitting racket of me playing was a far cry from young Jimmy's warm and soothing tones. So I laid the accordion down and wrapped the blankets around me.

I couldn't play the songs meself, but I could whistle 'em. And so I did. Only it was hard to keep the rhythm of

S.O.S. #7

Shiver Me Timbre, Yar, I'm a Pirate!

Oh, the sea is blue
And me heart is too,
Longing for the lass
With a love so true,
I pillaged 'n' I plundered
'N' now we're through,
Yar, I'm a pirate
That's what I do.

Her father is upset,
But what does he expect?
Stole her heart
'N' her diamonds
'N' her rings
'Cause treasure is
The most important thing
To a greedy thief like me.
Even knaves 'n' liars
Have dreams 'n' desires!
Oh, the sea is green
And so is me,
Jealous of the lad
With me ol' darling.
Battled 'n' we brawled,
Threw him to the sea.
Yar, I'm a pirate,
How else should I be?

Storms, they come and go,
So I hold on and hope.
Thunder rolls,
But the sky'll
Always clear.
One day soon
I will hold me dear
When I don't fill her with fear.

the music in time with the rumblings of me tummy. A few jelly beans later, the rumblings disappeared and the melodies were able to carry me off to sleep.

Another night with rough slumber and a horrible nightmare. I was sleeping next to Jimmy's accordion in the crew's chambers. (Ye may notice something funny about me jelly dreams. In fact, I just noticed it meself. Whenever I dream, it always starts off in the same place where I went to sleep!) And so the dream began. . . .

Thar was a strong wind rattling the sails. Even below-decks I could hear it clear as a bell. Finally, the wind would help me pick up speed, I thought. Upon closer listening, the wind started sounding like voices. It could have been none other than me no-good crew. I'd been certain as a sea snake is slippery they'd be back, and sure enough, they were. It didn't take long for the ole boys to see that First Mate McGee was no leader. I am the best captain to ever sail. They were lucky I was willing to take 'em back. Nice and neat, I tucked in me shirt and cleaned out me ears, then headed up to the main deck, ready to see me crew eager to take orders from a real captain once again.

That's when me dream turned into another nightmare. The only crew I found on deck was a crew of gigantic jelly beans. They were laughing and singing as, one by one, they waddled across decks and jumped back into the jelly bean barrel. I chased after them but they were all gone. When I looked in the barrel, the blasted beans were back to thar candy-sized selves. The dream didn't seem to be such a fright. Back to thar wee shapes, thar weren't much the mini-meanies could do in the way o' scaring me. Oh, how wrong I was, for the horror had just begun! When I turned to make me way back belowdecks, something awful caught me eye. Me sail had been ruined by a phony version of me sail painting, and a poorly drawn one at that. It turns me stomach to show ye what it looked like, but here it be:

The prank needed to be corrected right away. Not only did the jelly beans destroy me sails, but they also used up all me black paint. I did have a bucketful of red, so I took it off the mast and climbed the rigging. Seeing how I only had one bucket, I didn't really miss Boggs the Cabin Boy's help. A big red square on me sail would be a lot better than leaving the mess those jelly beans made. Actually, matey, this is where it *really* turns out to be a nightmare.

I dipped me paintbrush into the bucket and was shocked when I removed it. The red paint on the end of the bristles seemed so much brighter than usual. It wasn't long before I had half the mistake covered up with a brilliant square of red paint. It was so bright that me eyes burned. A very hot bright. Fire hot.

Thankfully, I can tell ye that at this point me nightmare was cut short. I woke from me dream, high up on the mast, coughing out clouds of smoke with a burning sail in front of me face! Wellington hobbled to and fro to escape the sparking embers invading his perch. I looked down to find that what I had thought was a bucket in me hand was actually a lantern. All along I had been painting the sail with fire! Without thinking, I tossed the lantern overboard and hurriedly climbed down the rigging to safety. Thar was no use trying to put her out; the fire had already spilled across the sail. The flaming canvas washed the deck below in a bath of red and orange light, and just as the sinister blaze was about to take over the whole ship, the air grew quiet. A fierce wind blew in like a cannonball and carried the burning sail away through the white curtain of fog.

I don't mind telling ye I covered me eyes in fright. I knew things weren't what they seemed. Li'l Whisker, have ye ever been given an apple for lunch? Red, shiny—delicious as can be. But ye bite into it only to discover the slimiest worm poking his head out of the sweet fruit. It seems like a good thing, only it goes rotten. I knew I was falling into the same kind of mess.

Now, every sailor worth his salt knows what happened to me. A Great-Grandpa Gust. It only comes once in a blue moon, but when it does, it rescues a sailor from a dreadful spot. And, Li'l Whisker, thar's always a heavy price to pay. After the wind comes to yer aid, it leaves ye changed into the thing ye hate most. Legend has it that one captain was so afraid of getting warts he took a nightly bath in pineapple sauce, honey, lamp oil and soap to make sure none would pop up on his body. One day a Great-Grandpa Gust blew him right out of a typhoon, and he wound up on the shores of an island. His crew said that just as he sank his hands into the moist sand, he turned into a big warty frog. According to the astonished men, before he hopped away his last two words were "rib" and "bit."

The old noiseless wind came after Shellfish Davey, too. He was caught in a terrible battle at sea and saw a cannonball coming straight for his galleon. Before he could warn his men about the dangers ahead, a Great-Grandpa Gust met the cannonball halfway and sent it back into the boat from whence it came. Three days later, Shellfish Davey woke up to find he was a one-hundred-four-year-old man. This story I know is true because I once sailed with Felonious fibber, who read the story himself in the *Pirate Picayune.*

As I stood watching the sail fly off into the fog, I could only guess what wicked fate the Great-Grandpa Gust had blown me way. I knew it would be the worst thing I could think of, which could only mean one thing: I would become a living, breathing jelly bean. And worse yet, I would probably be one of those green lime ones, yecch! Thar was only one way to keep the Great-Grandpa Gust from turning me into the thing I feared most. I had to make nice with those blasted—delightfully charming beans. The sooner I got back to sleep, the sooner I could make me new friends. I decided it was once again bedtime.

I grabbed a handful of jelly beans (thar were even a few green ones) and made me way belowdecks to me cabin. I swallowed the lot of 'em and fell fast asleep on the old treasure chest.

Ye get one guess where me dream began. That's right, in me cabin. With a smile on me face, I stepped out onto the deck. Sitting behind the wheel, I waited for them to show up. If ye think waiting around in real life is boring, ye should try doing it in a dream. It is really boring. It was so boring that I wanted to wake meself up. Then I remembered why I was thar. If I didn't make friends with them beans, I was doomed to become one.

Looking for something to do, I spied the fork stuck in the mast, so I popped it out and carved a game of tic-tac-toe in the deck to keep meself properly amused as I waited for the beans. Before I could scratch out the final "X" to win the round, I noticed a sugary scent pouring over me shoulder. It was a giant black bean breathing down me neck.

"Ahoy thar, Bean. Pleased to make yer acquaintanceship. What be yer name?"

The bean said nary a word. This friendship business was tougher than I thought. But I wouldn't give up easily. I tried once again: "Me name, good sir, is Cap'n Redbeard. How may I address ye?"

With narrowing eyes the bean finally responded: "I am Redbean."

"Har-har!" I laughed louder than I had laughed in ages. But when I looked at the bean, I knew he wasn't joking. "Pardon me for laughin'. It's just that I thought ye were havin' some fun with me name, that's all." Making friends is hard. Even harder than octopus wrestling. I decided to lighten the mood. Friends like to play games, right? Why couldn't this bean and I enjoy a little friendly fun? "Say thar, Redbean, what do ye say about a game of tic-tac-toe?"

Redbean's angry black face smiled just a wee bit.

"Sure, I'll play with ye, Redbeard. But if I win, an' I probably will, I get to take yer hat as me prize."

I kept reminding meself that it was all just a dream—he couldn't actually steal me hat. So I agreed to his bullish terms. And so we played. Three "X's" in a row won it for Redbean. (I let him win, and, to be honest, it felt good.) Without a thought, I reached up to surrender me hat, but as I did, he shook his giant jelly head. "No. That's not the hat I want." He chuckled in his bottomless voice.

I gulped. "Ye don't mean . . . ?"

"Aye, that's the hat I want. The golden one with the sapphires, and pearls, and a diamond the size of a chocolate-covered cherry. I want the crown of King Cornelius."

And with that, Redbean pushed his way past me right into the cabin. Like a spark I was after him. But even with speed on me side I was too slow. For when I caught up with him, me precious crown was already perched atop his dark head.

Me blood boiled quicker than me beard bristled. The crown I stole was stolen! Me new friendship was over before it even began. Matey, I learned a valuable lesson in that dream. If yer going to make some friends, pick some friendly ones, not a bunch of no-good, blasted, tooth-rotting, dream-ruining, ship-wrecking jelly beans.

Redbean snatched the crown from his head. Back and forth he tossed me treasure 'tween his candied hands. His pinhole eyeballs peered at the cabin window. . . . Me heart went squish when I saw that it was open.

Fie on Redbean!

"Redbean, hear me loud an' clear. Ye can come into me dreams and make me tear up me only map. Ye can trick me into paintin' me sail with fire. But nobody, but nobody, and I mean nobody, gets away with wearin' the crown I so dearly treasure. Ye, sir, are a bad bean."

I could stand the sight of him no longer. I decided it was time for the nightmare to end.

With a pinch on me earlobe, I woke up angry and pinching me earlobe. Across me forehead, me anger vein surfaced. That's how I know when I'm really angry and not just miffed. I had had it with the beans, so me rage lead me to the cannon. Thar was no way I could let it go on any longer. I needed to get rid o' them candies once and for all.

The crew had left me only one cannonball, but one was all I needed. After loading it into the shaft, I wheeled the cannon into position, facing the dreaded jelly bean barrel. Hunched over, I lit the wick. I didn't realize it then, but when I knelt down, some of the beans spilled out of me pocket. As I rose to watch the cannonball shoot through the fog, I slipped on a handful of the candies. Quite a thud was created as me whole body landed on the cannon, knocking it off target and sending it rolling down the deck. Straightaway, I saw that it was heading for the wheel. Before it stopped rolling, a boom echoed through the fog and wooden shards filled the air. The thinning smoke revealed a sad sight, me friend. The wheel was gone! The beans had fooled me in me sleep before, but this was madness. Now they had actually driven me to blow up me own wheel while I was awake.

Li'l Whisker, you can see that the beans left me in a sorry state indeed. They destroyed the *Picaroon* in every way short of sinking her entirely. I don't mind telling ye, but don't tell anyone else: for the first time in all me years at sea . . . I was lost. Thar was no telling which way was north or south or even stem from stern. What I wouldn't have given to set foot on dry land. I wonder if I would even have traded me crown to get off that ship. . . . No, no, no. That is shameful stuff for a pirate to wonder.

Maybe it was the bone-rattling sound of the cannon blast. It had been a very long time since the cannon was fired last. Did it scare Wellington away? Did he leave to search out me former crew? I didn't rightly know. What I did know was simple—the poor bird was gone! Facing the endless murk, I cried out, "Wellington! Wellington!" He was an old bird, so I worried. "It'll take ye too long to reach land. Ye'll never make it, ye fool!" By then I knew that wherever he was, he wouldn't even be able to hear me anymore. "Ye've sealed yer fate, me friend. Yer done for." Thar weren't a solitary thing I could do for the ole soul. Luck, 'n' luck alone, would have to keep a weather eye out for him.

I began to pick up the wheel's pieces. Its splintered wood littered the farthest corners of the deck. One of the helm's spokes had landed squarely on a brown crate, and as I reached to pick up the debris, I was struck by the memory o' the crew huddled around the big box for thar nightly arm wrestling matches. Of course, back then I never competed meself, seeing how it was obvious I was the strongest man on board. Every last crew member knew it was true, but blazes, not even I knew which one o' me musculated arms could outmuscle the other. I tossed the spoke to the floor planks, took a seat at the crate, and let me arms have at each other. Oh, what a tussle they had! The struggle went on for the better part of half an hour before I had to call it a draw. Even though the match turned out to be a tie, it would have been so much more exciting with me crew thar behind me, what, with all their whooping and hollering. I felt so bad for the *Picaroon;* she'd never been so quiet and alone.

S.O.S. #8

Out of Arm's Way

Thar, in the foggy darkness that had been sailing around me for I don't know how long, I drifted off to sleep. . . .

In the morning when I woke up, I knew for sure it was the dawn, and guess how I was so sure. Because the sun threw down its freshest golden rays that only come out in the earliest hours of the day. To be honest, I'm not sure if that was the very next morning, but I'm certain those were the first rays of light me eyes had seen since page thirty-two, when I lost me fishing pole.

Feeling the warm sun on me face blessed me belly with laughter. Finally I had enough energy to get meself out of that frightful pickle. Thanks to the clear skies, I could see all the way to the ocean's farthest reach. So I made use of the opportunity to scan the calm waters for a ship that might rescue me. By thunder, what me eyes fell upon was better than a whole fleet of rescue ships. An island! Not more than fourteen cannonball hops off the port side. Right away, visions of pineapples and sandy beaches rushed to me with a speed to make lightning bolts jealous. With any luck, the island would have people. But since I couldn't go to them, they would have to come to me.

"Land ho!" I cried out to that drop of land caught just below the horizon.

"Greetings, my good man."

Ye can imagine how shocked I was to get an answer. "Jolly good to hear another voice. Could ye be so kind as to help an honest sailor caught on board a doomed ship?"

"At your service, Captain."

At that, I realized something was fishy. "Wait a blasted minute. Yer voice ain't comin' from that island. Just where are ye at?"

"Right behind you. On the starboard side."

I turned and advanced to the opposite railing but I saw nothing. "I can't—"

"Down here! I'm in the water."

I lowered me eyes to the lapping waves and saw a beautiful woman swimming right alongside the *Picaroon*. It was strange enough to see a lady all alone in the ocean, but stranger still, she had a lovely headful of hair the color of coral. "Ahoy thar, young miss! Yer sweet voice sounds familiar. Might it come from the same mouth that spoke to me when I was trapped in the fog?"

"You aren't the first sailor to recognize my voice."

"Either way, I would be ever so grateful if ye could help me. Me ship is of no use, and I desperately need to get to yer island off yonder."

The li'l lady smiled and lowered her head back into the water. When she did, a burst of bubbles rose to the surface and shot into the air. I watched 'em rise until she came back out of the water and called up to me. "What island are you talking about?"

Pointing off in the distance, I announced: "Right behind me. Thar's a piece of land not too far off. Fer the life of me, I can't imagine ye'd come from anywhere else without any ships nearby."

Quickly she lowered her head back into the water. And again a burst of bubbles shot into the air and floated toward the sky. I didn't rightly know what to make of it. When she came back out of the water, I started to ask about her li'l routine, but she spoke before I could make so much as a peep.

"Maybe you should take another look, puzzled pirate."

As I turned around, that tiny island spread its wings, rose off the water and vanished behind a string of pearly white clouds. Matey, that isle was me only chance to get off the *Picaroon,* and it turned out to be nothing more than that no-good deserter, Wellington the Pelican! Me pirate skills were slipping. Not too long before, I could have spotted a bilge rat on the rigging of a distant ship. What a joke I'd become.

"Don't feel bad, pirate. Things aren't always what they seem. Sometimes you have to take a second look. At first glance, you thought I was a lady, right?"

"Aye, indeed I did. But ye are a missy, ain't ye?"

Her giggles poured out again. "Not exactly, Captain Redbeard."

Fear filled me boots as I questioned her: "How do ye know me name?"

As if to answer, she sank below the surface and a shimmering green tail fanned out from the salt water. Without a thought I shouted back, "Impossible! Mermaids don't exist!"

But thar she was, afloat on the sea, the green fin of a

fish attached to the body of a beautiful young woman. Her tail made terrific splashes in the water, swaying her hair away from her shoulders. It was then that I saw the fancy necklace she was wearing. It made me mouth water, seeing how it was a giant cluster of grapes wrapped all the way around. Her voice spiraled up, cheery and sunny-orange sweet. "My name is Rosetta. I was born to Delilah and Rutherford Slocum in a quiet home just beyond Neptune's Divide—a place known to you, of course, as the Barrier Reef. As you can see, I am as real as can be, Redbeard."

I shook me head. "Ye, me dear mermaid, are fake! I suppose ye think blowin' bubbles in the air makes ye some kind o' mermaid. Well, it don't!"

"For your information, Redbeard, that's the only way a mermaid can laugh, by sticking her head underwater."

"Nice try, missy, but I don't buy into yer two-bit legend. Yer a figment o' me imagination, just like that blasted Redbean. The only reason ye know me name is because I know me name."

"I don't understand. Who's Redbean?"

"It's not a matter o' who but o' what is Redbean. For he ain't no human, that's for sure. Redbean is that bad bean from me nightmares. I've already taken the liberty of pinchin' meself, so thar be no doubt here that I'm wide awake. But with the hunger in me belly and the tired in me bones, I still can't be trustin' me own eyes and ears."

"Is that what I look like to you—a nightmare?"

"Li'l miss, I've imagined ye, against me will, as the loveliest mermaid o' the deep. Unfortunately, that makes ye no closer to being real. I've never seen a mermaid, nor will I ever because they simply don't exist. Ye were completely dreamed up in me head—every last scale."

A stern expression overtook the young missy's pleasant face, and she raised her giant fish end high in the air, only to smack it with a tremendous force against the waves. I was soaked. Water spilled out from the brim of me hat.

"Captain, do you believe that? I splashed you. Or was it fake, just like me?"

Even with me beard dripping wet, I stuck to it. "It's all made up, just like ye. I haven't eaten a bite o' anythin' but jelly beans in ages, so I've fallen sick from the sweetness. Me mind is playin' tricks on me, that's all."

"Tell me this, Captain: if you don't believe I'm real, then why do you have a mermaid figurehead on your ship?"

"If ye must know, li'l lady, it came with the ship, which was a gift, and the only reason I've kept it thar all these years is so it can remind me that ye and yer kind don't exist!"

"Don't worry, Redbeard. I know humans don't believe in mermaids, but I'm as real as you. If it makes you feel any better, there are things that even mermaids don't believe in."

"Like what?"

"If you don't believe that I, a mermaid, am right here in front of your face, it's doubtful that you'll find the truly wondrous things worth your time."

"Time's no longer a treasure I can squander, so out with it, if ye please, miss."

"There's a place that every mermaid knows about, but none can say if it truly exists. An island surrounded by a magic so mysterious no fairy tale could contain it. It's a paradise filled with treasures beyond your wildest dreams."

Me friend, treasure is a subject near and dear to me heart. "Ye mean like gold and silver?"

"Not exactly."

"How about diamonds and pearls?"

"Well, for starters, this treasure is different. It is under every rock, caught in the vines of every tree, in the current of every stream. The island is alive!" Her eyes widened like she was looking at the island then and there.

"Well, what's it called? I've sailed the seven seas, so surely I've heard of it."

"Fundorado Island."

"I hate to disappoint ye, li'l missy, but thar ain't no such place."

"Oh, but I believe there is!" A smile spread across her face. "I've known the secret of Fundorado Island ever since I learned how to swim."

"So spill it."

"Not so fast, Redbeard!" She looked right at me like I had done something wrong. "If you aren't going to admit that I'm a real mermaid, then you aren't going to hear my story."

"Look, dearie, once and for all, it's high time I decided what happens in me imagination. So if I want to hear the story, then ye best be tellin' it."

Below the sea a dark cloud approached the *Picaroon.* The mysterious lady dipped under the water as the mass moved closer. Soon a school of fish swam right past her, hundreds of them all around. She stroked the bellies of those that trailed behind, then broke the surface of the water with her head. "You really can't believe what's right in front of your own eyes? Fine, Redbeard, if that's how it is, then I'm not going to let a single word about any treasure slip from my lips until you admit that I am real."

Li'l Whisker, me patience with this figment of me imagination was growing thin. Rather than argue with her, I decided on a good old-fashioned trusty double-cross. So I slipped me husky hand behind me back, crossed me fingers and put on a smile. "All right, then, ye win. I give up. So go ahead with yer story."

"Not until you say I'm real."

"Well, ye say ye are, don't ye?"

"Yes, but I want to hear you say it."

"Fine. So yer a real mermaid. Thar it is." Not only did I say what she wanted to hear, but I threw in a li'l wink for good measure. "I hope yer happy, li'l miss. Now out with the story of the treasure."

She took in me words, softly staring me down. Her glance dropped to the water, then returned to me. "It started long ago, before the earth learned how to spin. Two shooting stars whizzed through the night, sparkling across the sky, and just like that they went crashing right into each other. And do you know what happened, Redbeard? The stardust came tumbling down through the clouds all the way down to the ocean—so much stardust you can't even imagine! It kept raining down until it rose above the surface of the water.

"When the stardust settled into place, it longed to be much more than just a stretch of land in the middle of the ocean. So out of the glittery rocks a tiny green shoot reached for the skies. Slowly it unraveled and grew higher and higher until one day it was a full grown wamumass tree. Under the tree, where its shadow was cast, a thick patch of grass and a mushroom emerged. This island was good at growing. After quite some time, other plants and trees and flowers in wild gardens began to grow. And they kept growing. Fundorado filled itself with fantastical things the world had never seen."

"Like what?"

"Hold on, Redbeard! This story's over!"

"Ye can't quit now, ye—" Li'l Whisker, I couldn't even finish me own thought, for I realized that in the excitement of the moment I had whipped me husky hand out from behind me back, revealing me crossed fingers. I tried to slowly slip 'em back behind me. "Will ye kindly continue with the story?"

"Not so fast. I saw your fingers. I should have known not to make a deal with a double-crossing pirate."

"Yer right, missy. Let it be a lesson—most pirates aren't worth thar salt. Now that I've taught ye the lesson, we can start trustin' each other from this very minute." I revealed me hands again and dangled all ten of me uncrossed digits out in front so she could see 'em clearly.

"We can start trusting each other when you stop calling me missy. You know very well, Redbeard, that my proper name is Rosetta."

"Right ye are again, Rosetta."

"That's better. And would you be so kind as to keep your hands in front of you?"

"Don't worry, dearie—um, Rosetta. These hands o' mine aren't goin' anywhere so long as ye've got a story to finish." Of course, she didn't know that me boots were half a size too big, giving me just enough room to cross me toes on both feet. It weren't easy keeping me balance, so I leaned up against the railing with me hands where she could see 'em.

"If I catch you doing something like that again, Redbeard, I'll swim away and you'll never see me again."

"No worries, li'l miss. I'm not budgin'. I'd be a fool to walk away from yer story now."

"Keep calling me little miss and I'll swim away."

"Apologies again, Rosetta."

She took a moment to gather herself. It looked like she was starting back into her story, but she stopped herself again. "Redbeard . . ."

"Yes."

"How about your toes?"

"I beg yer pardon?"

"You heard me. I want to know why you're crossing your toes."

"How'd ye know about my toes?"

"I'm a mermaid, Redbeard. There are just some things we know. Mermaids can see things that humans can't."

"Oh, and I suppose that makes ye real, does it?"

"You can't always assume you know everything just because you're some bully of a captain. As they say down at Full Moon Reef, the ocean is always just a little bit deeper than you think."

"Fair enough, I'll uncross me toes, but only so we can get to the end o' this story of yers about the imaginary island." (Li'l Whisker, I did uncross me toes, but I want ye to know it wasn't because she told me to do so. Yer good friend Captain Redbeard has a bad case of bunions, and keeping me toes crossed only made the pain worsen.)

Rosetta raised her head and peered at the side of the boat. It almost looked as if she was seeing straight through the wood of the *Picaroon* and the leather of me boots to make sure me toes were straight. When she was satisfied, she nodded and cleared her throat. "It isn't an imaginary island. It's real. Now, where were we?"

"Fallin' stars and all kinds o' life springin' up on Fundorado."

"Right. Well, ages after the night of the falling stars, when humans walked the four corners of the earth, one curious group of people took to the great seas. And it was splendid timing, for at that moment our little island was full of jungles just teeming with magnificent creatures. Fundorado was full grown and ready for the people who spilled out onto its shores. At long last, all the island's adventures were to be explored."

"Well, who were these people? They weren't pirates, were they?"

"No, Redbeard."

"Are they still thar?"

She was growing impatient. "Captain, I'll get to that part. Hold your sea horses. The people lived in bliss but the tide soon changed. One night when the air was filled with the people's music and laughter, a jealous beast crawled out from his deep, dark dwelling."

"Was it a tiger?"

"No, Redbeard, it was worse—"

"A two-headed tiger?"

"Worse still. In fact, it was the worst creature to ever menace human beings. Its name was Fernobarb. The island had always been its home, and it had no intention of sharing with the people. So on that night the monster destroyed their boats and cast them into the depths of the ocean with its mighty fury of thunderbolts and its nightmarish tempest tantrum."

Fearing I knew the answer, I gulped and asked Rosetta, "What happened to 'em?"

"They were surely doomed, but Fundorado rescued the poor souls with its sparkletricity."

"Sparkly—what now?"

"Sparkletricity, Redbeard. As the humans struggled to keep afloat, their legs joined together in the form of brilliant fish tails. Slowly they gathered under the deep blue breakers and realized they had been transformed into the world's very first mermaids and mermen. The island saved them."

"Say fer a moment I think yer story's true—which I don't, but if I did—why don't ye and yer merfolk just go back to that sparkly island o' yers?"

Her voice was a little sad as she answered, "Because, Redbeard. Fernobarb made sure that could never happen. He's still there! And every day he raises a storm out of the surrounding waters where he circles, guarding his refuge day and night. Each crack of lightning and every icy raindrop is spurred by his possessive nature. The waves rage so fiercely that not even a mermaid can escape the current and break through to the calm paradise on the other side."

Even though her story was good, I didn't believe it. And I still didn't believe that she was a mermaid because even fools know they don't exist.

S.O.S. #9

A Fish Tale Review

Her story weren't all bad. In fact, I kind of liked it. It moved along quickly, had a great hook in the beginning and plenty of fancy characters sprinkled throughout. Maybe just a touch too jumbled. But all in all, not a bad yarn. I give it 4 out of 5 starfish.

"Rosetta, like I said in the beginning, yer a figment o' me imagination. I don't want to hurt yer feelins, but it's time fer me to stop imaginin' ye." So I squished me thumbs deep into me eyes until the bright spots and purple swirls twirled, but alas, when I opened them again she was still thar, tail and all. I closed me eyes again and shook me head like a wet dog. No luck. I bit me tongue, pinched me arm and spun around, but that mermaid was a tough vision to lose.

"Stop spinning around, Redbeard. You're going to make yourself sick. You don't need to prove that I'm fake. I'll show you that I'm real. I'll grant you any wish you want. Go ahead, make one."

"Hardy-har-har," I laughed. "Mermaids, a magical island, free wishes—ye expect me to fall fer that stuff?" Who'd she think I was, Boggs the Cabin Boy? "Oh sure, I could make a wish for me whole crew to return to the deck o' the *Picaroon,* but wishin' for somethin' that won't come true, now, that's a waste o' me time."

As I turned to make me way belowdecks, she hollered, up to me, "You're right, Redbeard, the jig is up. You don't have to believe in anything I've told you, but you might want this back."

Out of the corner of me eye I spied a golden glimmer. In the palm of her hand was the lost key to me beloved treasure chest! "How did ye . . . ? Where did ye . . . ? What did . . . ?" I stammered, and she tossed the key up over the railing onto the deck, where it landed with a quiet chime against me boot. Kneeling down to pick it up, clutching it in me fist, I discovered that the key weren't no illusion—it was real.

Raising her head out of the water, the mermaid whispered, "If you trust it even just a little bit, maybe one day you will believe the whole story." After she slipped below the seafoam I headed to me cabin with me precious key safely in hand.

Thar be not a sliver of fact to that mermaid's fiction. I learned long ago that running after fantasies gets ye nothing but an ache in yer side.

Matey, listen good 'n' hard to me words. Thar be something ye need to know, and it ain't easy for me to tell ye. But before I breathe a word, I need yer promise that ye can keep it secret. And if yer not one to keep secretive issues under yer hat, then I need to ask ye to kindly close me logbook and read not a word further.

Squealers, rats and betrayers, this story be over.

The End.
(Close the book.)

I’m serious.

Li'l Whisker, it brings a song to me heart to know I can trust ye. Now all I need is yer solemn oath.

Hold me logbook in yer right hand. Place yer left hand over yer left eye and please read aloud the following declaration (No crossing yer fingers—or yer toes!):

I, Li'l Whisker, do hereby promise to keep
Redbeard's secret under lock and key
For two days past forever and eternity.

And if ye break yer word of secrecy, yer punishment will be as follows:

Ye have a few choices. Ye can pick five burdens from category #1, two burdens from category #2, or one burden from category #3. Otherwise, pick three burdens from category #1 and one burden from category #2. Lastly, ye can pick one burden each from categories #1 and #2 if ye also take on a hearty burden of yer own design. (Make sure yer punishment fits the crime!)

#1 Lily-livered Landlubber Burdens

Burden 1: Eat three rotten sardines.

Burden 2: Take a two-day bath, including one hour of behind-the-ears scrubbing.

Burden 3: Eat five cookies but ye get NO milk.

Burden 4: Learn how to play the accordion.

Burden 5: Put pickles in yer lemonade.

Burden 6: In relation to Burden 5, if ye like pickles in yer lemonade like Googler, put eggs in the lemonade.

Burden 7: No pumpernickel bread for one month!

Burden 8: Stand on yer head and think about what ye did.

Burden 9: Run around the street with yer long johns tied around yer head.

Burden 10: Promise never to squeal again.

#2 Brave-Hearted Buccaneer Burdens

Burden 1: Get an "I Love McGee" tattoo.

Burden 2: Paint a fence 'n' whistle it dry. (If ye can't whistle, hum.)

Burden 3: Do all yer homework, feed it to the dog, then do it again.

Burden 4: Dress up like a rat, 'n' when yer mateys ask ye why yer dressed like that say, "Because I can't handle the responsibility of a secret."

Burden 5: Every night before bed, kiss an ice block for ten minutes to tighten up those loose lips o' yers.

#3 Unimaginable Burdens

Burden 1: Eat a whole barrel o' jelly beans.

Now that I have yer solemn word (and ye know what yer punishment be if ye break it), I can tell it to ye straight. . . . Matey, 'tis a sad but true fact that yer good friend Redbeard never had a mum and dad of his own. (As for me pappy, ye only get one secret at a time, so don't think I'll be givin' that to ye now.) From the time I was a li'l whisker, I was at sea, moving from one ship to another, one port to the next, never really knowing what it'd be like to hear the sweet voice of a mum singing me to sleep at night, or the soft palm of her hand against me cheek as I drifted off to dreamland.

When I was a boy, I might not have ever thought much about it if I hadn't been made to listen while the pirates told stories about thar homes and thar mums, memories of land and all the home cooking they used to enjoy. I'd be lying if I said it weren't hard to sit thar and listen to all that the older fellas had to say. What I wanted more than anything was to be able to tell me own stories about me own mum.

So one night I was with a crew docked in Turtle Bay. Out in the distance Scurvy Rock reached toward the sky under the moonlight. The men made their way down into the galley and Shellfish Davey asked me where I hailed from. (I didn't much care for Shellfish, but I was nice to him all the same, seeing how I had already sailed once with his uncle, Jonah, who buttered me up with his Deep-Sea Salmagundi.)

"Can't rightly say," I mumbled as I scratched at the peach fuzz on me face. "Spent me whole life at sea. No recollection o' me family or me home. All I know for sure is that I didn't have a mum under the same roof because . . . well . . . me mum is a mermaid. And she spends her days swimmin' deep below the surface o' the deepest waters."

Thar was a moment of silence, all eyes on me; then Shellfish Davey led all the men in a hearty round of laughter. "Oh, Purty Ferdy, ye are a funny cabin boy indeed." (No, Li'l Whisker, I ain't proud of what they used to call me, but for honesty's sake, I must tell it to ye straight.) "Ye sure can spin a good yarn."

"But it's true! And I'll prove it to ye!"

"Okay, Ferdy, ye best prove it."

"Well . . . well—" I stammered. "Ask Cap'n Shalwart. He was me first captain when I wasn't but seven years old. He told me I was such a good sailor I must have come from the sea. He reckoned I must be at least half merman. Besides, me mum comes to visit me."

"Does she now?"

"Yes! She knows where I am at all times—no matter the sea. And she finds me adrift. She bids me hello and we wave to each other. Once she even brought me two fistfuls o' giant pearls."

I wasn't helping meself in the least. Not only did the men still not believe me, but they threw themselves into a deeper fit of laughter, falling over each other with thar mugs in hand. I stood up and started to storm out o' thar. Shellfish Davey stopped me. "All right, Purty Ferdy, we'll believe ye. Soon as yer mum shows up with all 'em riches. Ye just give us a shout and we'll be right thar."

It goes without saying, Li'l Whisker, that I didn't get much sleep that night. I lay under me blanket with me eyes closed, and quietly, under me breath, I asked me mum to come find me. Wherever she was, I wanted her to show her beautiful face so all those no-good swabs would see and believe.

The next morning Shellfish Davey was hovering over me with sheer fright in his eyes.

"What is it?" I asked him. "Ye look like ye've seen a ghost!"

"I might as well, Purty Ferdy." He ran his rugged hand down his face, trying to rub the shock out of his eyes. "It was Stink Pot. He was on lookout in the crow's nest. Right at sunrise he spotted her."

"Spotted who? Who did he see, Shellfish?"

He could barely bring himself to say it. "It's yer mum. She's out thar. Sittin' plain as day up on Scurvy Rock!"

Nary a word can tell ye how me heart leapt, Li'l Whisker. I put on me boots and shot up to the deck with Shellfish Davey right behind me.

The crew was gathered, staring off into the distance. Stink Pot grabbed me by the arm and pointed out to Scurvy Rock. "Look, Purty Ferdy! Thar she be! I couldn't believe me eyes when I saw her."

I leaned over the railing and squinted across the tide. And thar she was, silhouetted just in front of the sun still rising above the water. Without a second's hesitation I leapt onto the railing and dove into the water.

Never did I swim faster. Me arms couldn't swing high enough and me legs couldn't kick hard enough. As I went along, I tried to steal a glance at her but the water kept splashing in me eyes. Closer and closer I went until finally I hoisted me tired, soaking wet body up onto the rock. It was then that the worst sickness filled me stomach, me whole chest—every bone in me body. Li'l Whisker, it weren't me mum. It was nothing but a giant dead sea bass, rotting away, wrapped up in a mound of seaweed. In the middle of the tangled green web was a small piece of paper with a single sentence: "Welcome home, Purty Ferdy, me favorite son." I recognized Shellfish Davey's writing. The ugliest penmanship of any pirate ever! I turned around and saw the crew standing at the railing, grasping thar bellies as all the laughter tossed thar stomachs up and down.

It was then that I knew for sure: thar be no way for mermaids to exist. Not in any sea. Nowhere. Never.

I wiped the salty drops from me eyes and dove back into the water. It was the longest swim of me life, heading back to the ship.

Now that we have me deepest secret out of the way, we can move on with the rest of me story. And don't ye worry, Li'l Whisker, from this point forward, ye can tell anyone in the world the details o' me adventure. But remember, not a word about me mum!

Down in me cabin I sat. Me key was back, sure, but now I had a lot o' strange thoughts circling round. Ye see, some things just are, and other things, no matter who ye be, just aren't. It made me dizzy trying to figure out why me brain wanted to confuse the two. It's some rotten imagination I have, sending a mermaid to play games with me mind. "Rosetta, wherever ye are, I have me fingers crossed that ye can hear me words. I don't want to be too much of a brute, but yer not welcome back. It's dangerous to give a man hope that he can't use. Yer a nice enough figment, it's just yer stories that are cruel. To be honest, yer company went well with me loneliness, but yer tall tales were too much. So no longer can ye come here, fillin' me ear with the ill o' pretend. Swallow yer words, missy; I'm not lookin' for somethin' to believe in. I have everythin' I need to believe right here."

It had been a long time since I had donned King Cornelius's crown. I'd like to tell ye exactly how long, but I had lost track of the days. Oh, how I longed to wear it upon me head once again. Passing the golden key from hand to hand, I sat in front of the old sea chest. I had already gone without me treasure for quite some time, and I wondered just how long I could last. It made no matter; once again the key was mine, and it was time to wear me crown. As I moved to unlock the trunk, I was frozen by an unsavory feeling—the feeling of nothing. The *Picaroon* seemed to have stopped moving. Stowing the key under me hat, I made a dash up top.

Li'l Whisker, I stood thar in the middle of the deck searching in every direction and I couldn't find a single swell. The skies were abandoned and the sea was dead still—no waves, no currents. Maybe it had turned to ice. To test me notion, I palmed a few jelly beans and flicked one to the slick surface.

With a bloop the tiny bean sank into the deep. Its ripples lapped against the bow and danced out toward the horizon farther than I could see. It was a stillness the likes of which I had never felt. The calm was defeated when a golden lightning bolt tore from the lonely skies. Drops of rain soon followed, and without warning they turned into sheets, flooding the upper deck of the *Picaroon.* A frigid wind unraveled from on high and charged at me from all directions. I couldn't take a single step; I was locked in place. I tried to move again and again but each time it was no use.

Woken from its unusual sleep, the great sea stirred, bucking madly, almost tossing the ship to the storm-churned sky. The wind and rain whipped into me as booming thunderclaps echoed above, and then, in a flash brighter than two stars colliding, a lightning bolt crashed into the stern of the *Picaroon.* Sparks streaked up from the back of the ship, and in the smoke that billowed forth I could smell the stench of charred wood. With all the strength I could muster, I fought the storm with every step 'n' inched me way over to see what damage had been done. After clearing the smoke I could see it. Below the back railing the bolt from the sky had chiseled a single burned slash between the "R" and "P," spelling certain doom: "R-I-P." This was dreaded news for all on board the *Picaroon* . . . namely me.

S.O.S. #10

For Sail

Pirates, like most folks, have traditions, and the traditions of buccaneers may seem funny to landlubbers. One of me favoritest traditions as a captain was to sail up the Atlantic along the southwest coast of Ireland. From Crook Haven past Dingle Bay and all the way around to the cozy cluster of the Seven Hogs Islands we would travel, taking in the purty scenery and of course the port towns' riches too. So successful were our plunderings, we decided to make the looting trek at the beginning of every season. We'd stop at Crook Haven, venture north to the Seven Hogs and then return to Crook Haven for one last hurrah. Believe it or not, Crook Haven actually went by the name of Wiltingshire before me band of wicked scoundrels made it our favorite town to pillage. In those days we sailed in the *Vulgaris*, a decent ship, although a wee bit small and sluggish against the tide. The *Vulgaris*'s biggest problem was that it wasn't scary enough for me liking.

One year when summer sprang early, I was marching through the streets of Crook Haven when the mayor, Liam O'Sheen, rushed up to me with the most remarkable offer. He swiped the floppy hat from his head and wrung it between his fists. "Excuse me, Mr. Beard, might I have a word with you?"

Quite odd it was to have the mayor approach me. I found it to be most amusing and I let him continue. "Uh, yes, well—Captain, I have a unique offer for you . . . um, involving . . . well . . ."

Close enough to bite him in half, I stepped right up to his cherry face. "Out with it, ye swine!"

"Right. Quite right." He gulped three swallows down into one and let out his entire thought. "We the citizens of Crook Haven have taken note that you do indeed like to plunder our good town no fewer than four times a year, usually at the start of every season. As you may realize, this behavior of yours is certainly bad for the business of our shopkeepers and townsfolk. So the Town Hall has decided to make you an offer. Our best shipwrights and craftsmen have gotten together to design a pirate ship to end all pirate ships. It's tight at the bow to cut through the waters at a blinding clip. The deck is broad enough for a circus act and the whole ship is gloomily painted the color of ash. We have dubbed the maritime masterpiece the *Picaroon*, and the letters "R" and "P" (as in "Redbeard's *Picaroon*") have been expertly carved at the rear for admiration from behind. The best part is it's all yours! Mr. Beard, I can honestly say you won't be disappointed."

Me brain stalled at the thought of this helpless town presenting me with such a gift. "And, me good mayor, why, may I ask, are ye givin' a ship to me?"

"It's a trade-off of sorts." He forced a nervous smile between his words. "We give you the *Picaroon* in exchange for your raiding our town of Crook Haven but once a year instead of four times."

The concept made a boatload of sense. It wasn't too much to ask. With a shake of our hands the deal was sealed. I stuck to me word and like a true gentlemen invaded the little village only once a year—usually in the spring.

Thar were no signs of the weather easing up, so I made a retreat to me cabin as more flashes ignited in the distance. This weren't no natural storm.

While I was in me quarters, the ocean threw itself into a fit, hurling the boat onto its side. I lost me footing 'n' slammed into the wall, falling to the foot of me heavy treasure chest. The ship heaved again, knocking the painting of me first raid to the floorboards.

Now, here's a dashing fragment from me favorite painting.

If I couldn't save the *Picaroon*, then the least I could do was save meself. Thar weren't no time to spare. I sprang the chest open, emptied it of its coins and ripped out the secret door hiding the crown. The lock had some bite on the key; no matter how I tugged, it wouldn't come loose. I had to take cover quick, so I hunkered down. Thankfully, thar was just enough room for me to ride out the storm in safety.

In the trunk, I sat balled up around me crown. A slice of light peeked through the space between the key and the keyhole, and it flickered in time with each growl of thunder. As the ship rocked, the chest slid across the floor, ramming into the wall. Back and forth it went, taking me with it, pounding me into the sides. Trying to keep me wits about me, I counted each time the trunk was hammered against the wall. Eighty-five thrashings was as high as I got before the trunk hit with such a force that me head whipped forward, smacking into the crown. I tried desperately to keep me eyes open, but me mind turned fuzzy. I was done for. I could only count one more knock into the wall as I hunched over me treasure and slipped into the darkness.

Cradled in the trunk, I had many strange and wondrous visions, but even if I tied them all together and dreamed the whole thing twice, it wouldn't come close to what I was about to experience.

With a crash, the ship jolted to a halt, pulling me out of me slumber. The *Picaroon* had run aground. It was perfectly quiet outside, which meant I had successfully weathered the storm, but alas, I was still cooped up in the chest. I nudged the top o' the trunk with me elbow, but it wouldn't budge. Thar, stuck in the lock, I could see the key with rays of the sun casting an orange glow around it. I was locked in. Thar was no way out. I was about to lose all hope when I remembered the mermaid and the wish she had offered to grant me. It sounds silly, but me only chance of escape was to put that mermaid's wish to the test.

For the life of me I couldn't figure out how to make a wish, so I started concentrating really hard. Li'l Whisker, I've found that the best way to concentrate is to shut me eyes and squeeze me hands into tight fists. Well, after a while it started to feel like I was wishing, so I began to think about getting out of the trunk, over and over again. Loud bangs and thumps came from inside me cabin, and me trunk even began to quake about (I guess wishes can be a little noisy). When I felt that enough time had passed for the wish to come true, I opened me eyes up wide. Me key was gone! From the keyhole where it had been a brightness spilled in, drenching every ruby and jewel on me crown. Brilliant colors lit up the walls o' the cramped box and blinded me mercilessly. Again I reached up to try the lid, and to me amazement, it popped open—exactly as I had wished!

I sat up and slowly raised meself out of the trunk (I was awful cramped after sitting in such a tight spot for so long). I exhaled a long, wet pant over the crown's diamond, wiped the slickness clean with the sleeve of me shirt and locked me treasure away. Stumbling across me cabin to the window, I tried to rub the brightness from me eyes. When me sight came back, I looked through the gaping holes in the shattered stained-glass window of me cabin. Not only were me windows destroyed, but half the wall o' me chambers was missing! Me poor *Picaroon* would never sail again.

Outside, me eyes fell upon a mountain capped by the most strangely wonderful peak. To get a better look, I decided to make me way to the main deck. Getting out of me cabin proved difficult on account of the thrashing the room had taken from the crash. I even noticed that me king-sized hammock had been torn to tatters. The hole in the wall was blocked with dagger-like shards of wood, so I went the other way, lumbering past the debris on me way toward the companionway leading up above.

The *Picaroon* had set ashore on a slant much steeper than I had thought. After climbing over the railing, I hopped down into the soft sand and raised me head skyward. Shooting up behind a dense jungle, the giant mountain commanded me attention. At its base, sleek boulders were piled on top of each other with enough space for a rough trail to wind its way halfway up the jagged slope. The other end of the path disappeared into the mouth of a small cave. At the top of this cave a wishbone-shaped waterfall showered down, splitting into two halves on either side of the entrance. The base of the falls collected in a body of water that circled the top part of the mountain like a moat. Most miraculous of all was the source of the waterfall. It was hidden deep under the sparkling crystal top of the peak. Li'l Whisker, it was then that I knew without a doubt that thar at the top of the mountain were the hearts o' the twin stars Rosetta told me about.

I've heard plenty o' folklore, sat and listened to many a tall tale and spun a few yarns meself. But never had a story dared me to believe it as much as Rosetta's did now.

I was standing on Fundorado Island.

Looking down, I saw that I was on a curious beach. Me boots were firmly planted in brightly glimmering sand. Scooping up a handful, I let the stardust slip between me fingers. I smacked me hands clean of the polished powder and turned me ear to an unusual sound coming from where the *Picaroon* was beached.

Sharp cracks sounded through the breeze, echoing off the wooden planks of the ship. On a rocky ledge above the *Picaroon,* a tree was bowed over, nice and taut, its vines tangled in the rigging. The branches must have been caught up in the mast as the ship was forced ashore. *Snap!* The tree split apart at the base, and before I was able to leap, it toppled down, drumming into the deck.

In the shadow of the ship, I crouched, trying to protect meself from the sudden crash. No sooner had the tree collapsed than marble-sized pellets began raining down upon me head. Holding out me hand, I caught a few. They were a fruit I had never seen. I stuck 'em right in front of me nose and took a sniff. They had a sweet smell like a cinnamon roll, so I popped them in me mouth. Li'l Whisker, they were a tasty delight, and by the time I finished savoring the delicious morsels, I realized I was up to me knees in them. Me days of nightmarish jelly beans were over!

I spied a small feline creature as it tore out of the grass at the far end of the fallen timber up on the rocky ledge. The strange cat darted away in a blur with its unnaturally long tail streaming behind in the air. As I wiped me mouth of the gushing fruits' stickiness, I heard some more commotion up on the rocky ledge.

Through the scribble of branches I caught a glimpse of it: with a potato of a body on two stilt legs, it stood by the tree's broken base, one hand scratching its head—a head that flopped like an unfluffed pillow. Clutched in its other hand was a colorful staff that stretched just over its hair, with a long barb drooping toward the ground. The critter wasn't too large, just about the size of a sailor who fancies himself a tall person. Scattered across its plump rolling belly were rich brown speckles. (They showed up quite nicely against its rusty yellow hide. In fact, it looked not too different from a Cuban banana.) When it turned, I saw that it had a short gray mane with shocks of white hair stretching from the top of its lumpy head to the end of its drooping back. Its gangly arms flopped about as it picked through the wreckage the tree had left behind.

No doubt about it, this was most surely a bit too odd to be an animal—it was definitely a critter. I reckoned it could offer up a fair fight, but I was more than certain it wasn't Fernobarb, the dark beast that haunted Rosetta's tale, for this fella tripped about over its own cloaked charm.

In the dust, the critter knelt down and frantically peered into a couple of crude clay pots. Then it raised a

Me first impression of key thief 'n' cat.

ragged, painted cloth cover and searched the area for something that apparently didn't want to be found. As it leaned over, I noticed a frayed strand dangling from its neck. Can ye believe it, Li'l Whisker? Wheeling around at the end of that string was me very own key. How in blazes did that creation get a hold of it? The critter paused, rose up on its long thin legs and searched the surroundings again, its eyes filled with worry. Away it creeped, bunching its nose to take in any odors drifting in the air. It was slipping off, but not with the key to me treasure. A few fruits fell from the folds of me coat with each step I took from the *Picaroon*.

I sidestepped through some leathery branches, hot on the strange yellow critter's tail, and pushed me way out to a clearing. On the other side I found a faint path extending to the right and the left, curving away from the shoreline behind me and into the jungle. I looked both ways. Which direction did that spotted bugger choose? I cupped a hand to me ear and drifted off to the right. All I could hear were the chirping dips and vaults of the songbirds. There was not a sign of the key thief! At about fifty paces I decided it might serve me better to turn and head back the other way. (Turning around was just a hunch, really—but I'm always respectful of hunches.)

Me path, strewn with puddles and flickering stones, wound into a tight curve. The branches on either side were so dense I couldn't see a thing beyond 'em. That no-good creature had to be on the trail; I just hoped I chose the right direction. Flowers of bold blues and dusty maroons lined a gap in the high bush wall. A new road led off to the right, and, from the looks of it, doubled back just a wee bit. Overhead the trees crisscrossed, blocking most of the sun's light. Here the brush crept back, letting a tunnel slither its way into the overgrowth. O' course, the trail I had been following continued, but I couldn't resist a detour dotted with those lovely flowers. (Thar as big as plates, you know.)

Once in the jungle passageway, I realized it was an honest-to-goodness maze. I knew thar be many choices to be made: at a thorny rock the path forked, ending at the fuzzy trunk of a giant tree. The trail T-boned into another, 'n' behind a crusty pond, vines led over a mound of soil to yet another path. And still no trace of me key.

Li'l Whisker, I was turning left and right, ducking under and scaling over; and all the while, unbeknownst to me, I was getting meself good 'n' lost! At a patch of wet grass I knelt down and shook the sweat from the brim o' me hat. To keep from going down a path I had already traveled, I would mark my trail by piling rocks on one another. And so I ventured farther into the maze, looking for a way out.

I didn't have much luck. Surely I was going in circles, for every time I came to a turn or bend, I threw down yet another rock, and some of me stacks grew knee high. If I couldn't find me way out, I would try to fight me way out! I charged at one of the jungle walls and burrowed as far as I could get. I didn't get too far at all. The branches and vines were knit like a sweater. I dug deep, but the trees wouldn't give.

Smelling of buttery sap, I pulled out of the thicket and leaned over to land another stone on the pile. But this stone, it had a stubborn way. It bit the land and clung tight. For such a small stone it had a boulder's weight. I squatted over the rock, slipped me fingers in the soil and rolled the heavy nugget from its seat. And what came from the hole this rock was plugging? A swarm of bugs, Li'l Whisker. Beetle-sized flying fellas with a big hollow stern. Thar legs beat thar back ends, 'n' that's why I call 'em drumbugs. Up and around me they flew, thar ends thumping and clicking in a hypnotic rhythm. I dropped the stone to the ground and ran blindly for escape. As I ran they flew into me, pressing me firmly down the path.

Me arms flailed in the air. "Off me, now! Off me! Nunghhhk! Tttt-ttt! Tttt-ttt! Tttt-ttt!"

I sucked one of 'em into me mouth. It rattled 'tween me teeth. I spit it back out 'n' sealed me lips with a smirk. The drumbugs were guiding me out of the Jumbled Jungle. At forks 'n' splits along the path they'd nudge me in one direction, sweeping me down the trail. I stumbled through a batch of fat vines onto a misty plain. The sun was falling asleep; it simmered in jealous reds. The drumbugs circled round a few times before snapping 'n' popping back to the jumble's narrow corridors.

Behind the maze of dangly-branched trees and frizzy bushes circled a lifeless field of dirt. And far across the labyrinth forest was a long, tall hill. The mist fell featherlight into spurts of steam whistling over the expanse. Thar were fountains blasting up, oh, I'd say two and three men high, sending another sheet of mist down to the rugged ground. On top of the long ridge, motion caught me eye. The speckled fella stood cautious, staring me down.

"Wait right thar!" I growled as I rushed toward it.

Its staff jolted in shock. The critter took a few long strides to the top of the hill, then quickly vanished down the other side. This is where I got meself in a real pickle, not to mention the fact that I was starting to catch on to the fact that the yellow critter was playing me like a concertina. It led me right into the geyser field. I was gaining on the speedy devil when a geyser knocked me off me feet and whipped the hat clear off me head. 'Fore I could reach down to grab it, another geyser blasted it straight into the air and I stood thar jumping up and down till the spray stopped. I chugged forward, careful to dodge the gasping vents of peppery steam.

Roots looping from the soil helped me pull meself up the face of the hill. At the peak of the slope I caught a distant glimpse of that li'l devil, already at the base of a steep drop-off. The hill was saddled by a sturdy slab of rock, pooling with springs. As the pools filled, water flowed inside gouges all the way to the bottom. By thunder, that must have been how the key thief got down in such short order. Plugging me nose, I skipped over to the springs and cannonballed into a deep spot in the middle. From dimples in the floor of the pool, a warm current gently tugged at me, pulling until I slid down the face of the rock. Torrents of water were riding under and over me. Me vision was completely obscured by the pitching gushes, and I lost sight of the creature.

Fast over the rocky slope I tore. Me belt buckle squealed against the surface. The wet stone bulged out and I fell through the air into a collection pool. Me body drifted in a dance with the rough water. I reached for me hat and half swam to the shore. Far below, me toes sank into the steep embankment. I leaned forward to get a grip o' one of the vines dipping into the dark water.

Well! If it isn't how luck would have it. I grabbed the vine that grabbed back! In one motion I was hanging upside down with a spout of water emptying out me collar. I jerked me arms 'n' twisted like an angry eel. The vine wouldn't loosen its hold. I fought all night . . . mostly. If ever I woke up, I made sure to give the tree a li'l nibble, or even a pinch now and again. But I always fell right to sleep before I could do any good.

Day 2

The next morning I opened me tired eyes and tried to gather me senses. It took a while to remember exactly where I was, seeing how it was me first night of sleep on Fundorado. Li'l Whisker, it ain't easy realizing where ye are when yer away from yer beloved treasure, hanging upside down on a island you've never seen on a map, much less traveled with yer own two feet. Me first night was a hard one, to be sure. I wanted to get the day off to a good start. Me first order of business was getting me body out of the clutches o' the willow that had snatched me up.

I raised me heavy head to gauge me surroundings. With the sun rising, I was able to look up and see the vine still wrapped tightly around me husky calves. And I wasn't alone. Thar were dozens of trees around me, each of 'em with some prey wrapped up in thar thick vines. I looked toward the river and saw one of the willows closer to the bank move its vine down near the water. It hovered for a moment before it dove below the surface, snatched out a fish and raised it right up next to me. I realized that those willows were fishing willows. Every single one of 'em had some hearty breakfast tangled in its grip. Some had already eaten and were dropping the leftover bones to the ground. Others were still munching away, using thar oversized leaves to polish off the food. And some sat with vines dangling over the water, waiting for just the right

moment to pounce. It was good news for me, Li'l Whisker, seeing that these hungry stalks seemed to only like seafood. I almost felt sorry for the poor fella that snatched me up. Maybe it was me shark teeth that confused him. Understandable. He wasn't the first to confuse me with Black Finn, the fiercest creature of the sea.

I wiggled me toes and worked me feet back and forth, seeing how hard it'd be to turn meself loose. No sooner did I start to fussing than the tree's vine unfurled, sending me tumbling down to the mucky bank. I jumped to me feet and wiped meself clean. Only trouble was me left boot had slipped off me foot. I looked up and saw it still stuck between the leaves of the tree's vine. Thar were no way for me to retrieve it, seeing how I never learned how to climb trees. It always seemed like a landlubber skill and I never gave it me best effort. Besides, I could find a way to survive without me boot. If me journey to Fundorado taught me anything, it taught me that survival has a lot to do with cutting yer losses and moving forward. After staring straight into the soul of the Great-Grandpa Gust, Redbean and the like, I wasn't about to let a missing boot slow me down. (Even if the leather was cut from the killer bull I whipped while taking in some rest the summer before on the southern coast of Spain.)

I started back into the thick of the land, trying to find me way beyond the trees, maybe see if that speckle-bellied creature was anywhere in sight. Using yesterday's stacks o' stones, I was able to find me way through the jumble.

It's always easier to move more quickly when ye've gained a li'l history with the land. Although I did still need the help of those handy drumbugs to get me out o' the thickest stretch of the Jumbled Jungle.

I was feeling so good I even took a few detours, stumbling upon more wonders. I clambered up the side of a small cluster of hills to get a better view of the area. Up top, I realized the peaks were joined together by a series of strings. They looked sturdy enough to grab on to and shimmy yer way from one to the next. And down below, I saw li'l white creatures roaming around at the tops of the hills. They weren't any bigger than ole Wellington, but they had the most peculiar coats, with fur that stuck straight out like they had just had a good jolt. And thar heads were small and squarish, with tiny slits for eyes. Some of them were spinning more strings, while others hopped aboard the nearest piece of thread and rode it from one peak to the next. They were living up thar, using the strings as thar passages for traveling from one peak to the next.

I knew I outweighed the critters; still, I couldn't resist testing the strength of thar handiwork. So I grabbed hold of one o' them strings and started me descent down the far side of the hills. I almost made it too, but the line gave out just before I hit the ground. It snapped in me hands and I fell on me back. The critters were looking down at me from up top. I quickly rose to me feet, removed me hat and shouted up to 'em, "Ye have me apologies. I

Here be Munlots. Take a look at me wild thing roster for a laugh about how they reacted to the sound as I cleared me throat.

figured they looked strong enough fer a pirate. Maybe next time I'll double up for a li'l reinforcement." They stared for a moment longer 'fore going back to work.

Beyond the hills, I found meself moving through an open sweep of stones that were wide and smooth, like the ocean in the middle of a dead calm. The far side sloped straight down about a quarter of a mile and gave way to a curious series of old ruins. Remembering Rosetta's words, I surmised that this might have been the spot where the human folks lived ages before. And if that were the case, they were all long gone, for ye could tell by the sight of the place it hadn't been traveled in years. I looked down and in the center of it all were towering walls of ivy cascading down. At the sight of 'em, I stopped in me tracks, for it weren't just yer average ivy, ye see; it was the color o' deep burgundy. When I gave it a good look-over, squinting with all me might, I saw that the ancient walls held a funny kinda scribble writing, like the code to a secret language. Li'l Whisker, I had every intention of grabbing me logbook and making notes about the symbols I saw in front of me, but I had me priorities. It had been me first night away from the *Picaroon* since the day I claimed it as me own, and I couldn't wait another minute before heading back to me beloved treasure to make sure she was still safe and sound. So I continued through the stretch of stone, running along the edge with me hand shielding the side of me face so I wouldn't be tempted to look down at the ruins and think about stopping. I knew thar weren't no time to waste. I kept me mind busy by thinking about the curious stardust shore where me ship was sitting. It was special enough to give it me own personal name, so I decided to call it Spangled Beach.

And wouldn't ye know it, just as soon as I came up with that twinkling sand's name, I saw the shore in the distance. Thar the *Picaroon* sat, just like she was when I had left her the day before. I closed me eyes and took a husky breath, feeling better now that me ship was safely under me watch.

I took a stroll just above the *Picaroon* to investigate the broken tree. Ooze dribbled down the wounded trunk, pooling 'tween the roots. Around the tree, a camp of sorts was laid about, with an old fire pit, and a clay mug planted in the ash. Strangest of all were the images of unusual animals painted on the backs of long, flat leaves. There were more drawings to be seen, but I spied something worrisome down by the ship.

I knelt down and brushed me fingers against a large footprint. I could tell from the way it sank into the rock that it had been thar for a while, but I hadn't noticed it before on account of that yellow speckle-bellied critter distracting me. I looked around and saw that thar were several of the same footprints spanning the width of the cliff. Li'l Whisker, this was exactly what I was hoping I wouldn't find. Based on thar size and the creepy feeling brewing in me belly, I figured the tracks could only belong to Fernobarb. I needed to know for certain, so I raced down to the ship to grab me logbook and make a tracing of one of the imprints. Here it is, for yer own eyes. . . .

The dark shade on me sole is from a coating o' nectar.

I was squatting over the impression when a shadow soaked the open pages of me logbook. Terror had me as still as a stone. A weight fell against me shoulder, I jerked back, desperately trying to avoid the wrath of the barbaric beast. Twisting around to see who was thar, I recognized the lopsided head of that key-robbing yellow critter with his wide eyes staring down at me. Less than an arm's length away, the key hung just over me head. I grabbed for it, but as I moved, the critter sprang down the cliff 'n' into the sand. Scrambling to me feet, I charged at him. Oh, but how spry the scamp was, for as sure as I was that I could nab it, I was flying straight for the dunes. Me face was powdered with the island's brilliant sand. Again I rushed for it, and again I was much too slow. The critter stood not too far fom me, delicately playing with the key 'tween its fingers. As I had seen before, it bunched up its nose—this time shaping its mouth into a clever curve. "Won't hurt you," it taunted.

Li'l Whisker, ye should have seen the size of me eyes when I heard that the critter could talk. "What the blazes . . ." Me shout echoed, skipping from boulder to boulder across the cliffs above. "Ye . . . ye can talk!"

"Shush it up, you," the critter snapped. "This one makes human babble like you—but must have no voice now."

"But how in the—" I tried to toss the words out, but I found it near impossible, what with the speckled hand smothering me mouth. His lips were silent, yet his eyes spoke plenty, peering right through me like a schoolmaster spotting a cheat. I could be wrong, but I think those peepers were telling me to put a cork in it!

The grip of a squid wouldn't be as tight as his. He latched on to me arm and tugged me up the beach behind a curtain of curling fronds. Breaking the quiet, I blurted out, "Look here, ye swab, that purty bauble hangin' from yer neck is me key. Mine! I'm askin' for it nice—don't make me ask twice!"

"This one never said you could stop the hush." His voice shrank to a rasp. "The more shhh you make the safer you are. If Fernobarb hears you, you won't be happy." Glancing over his shoulder, he continued, "When that one finds you, it finds trouble too. This one wants none of that."

By the fishy smell of Neptune's armpit, thar was no way that a captain of me power would stand to let a speckle-bellied thing tell me when I could talk. I pushed me nose against his and railed at him: "Ye best watch who ye boss around, ye no-good barnacle. The next time ye think about stealin' something from me, try thinkin' about something else—like not stealin' from me!"

"Yummy, loud! Mmmm-mmmm, loud! That's what Fernobarb thinks of loud things. Loud things like the pirate man. Noisy snacks are that one's most favorite. If you don't like to get eaten"—he wrapped his words in a whisper—"be a quiet snack."

The li'l imp was in no need of sass, but his remarks did

raise a thought in me head. . . . With that terrible beast on the prowl, I realized I needed to move me belongings (namely, me treasure) from the *Picaroon* to a more hidden, secret-like location. Whispering through me beard, I made me point quietly and clearly. "Matey, I want that key. I won't be a very nice person until I get it back."

"Not a very nice person, you do that well, Beardface. Nothing is not as nice as destroying this one's home."

I never destroyed a home (on this island, at least). Like a bass's my mouth hung open in shock, my jaw dropping lower and lower as the critter's accusation unfurled: "You crashed the dark boat into the tree that fell over and made a crush out of the home. There is no more home for this one, so there is no more key for you!" He looked very pleased with his notion that somehow me key made up for the loss of his dwelling.

A blush came upon me cheeks, barely peeking over the mess of whiskers sprouting from the sides of me face. "A thousand pardons, I had no idea. Yer home is . . . gone, ye say?" I spoke the words, but me apology (possibly the first one I've ever truly meant) was answered by the creature slowly shaking his head to and fro.

"No more, human, my home is no more. The little house I made from mudtubes and fanroots is the same as the one you ruined with the big boat."

His sadness looked like it was shaping up to be one o' them contagious varieties, so I tried me darnedest to steer clear. "But, me friend, when me ship, the *Picaroon*, knocked the tree into yer home, I was locked up in a trunk. Clearly it weren't a thing I did on purpose. Don't ye, ah . . . ah . . ." His name, I realized, remained unknown. "What might I be callin' ye, matey?"

He rested his hands on his rolling belly and said, "This one is Marmoona."

"Well, the pleasure's mine, Marmoona. It's a mighty fine treat to meet such a spotted fella as yerself." I extended me hand in a friendly gesture, hoping he would offer his in turn. For a moment he pondered the introduction. "Put yer hand in mine. It's what friendly folks call a handshake."

Oddly enough, he knew plenty about shaking hands; he just didn't want to shake mine. "This one only shakes hands with friends." He showed a curiosity about me, asking, "A name for you?"

"Arr, me manners have escaped me. The name be Cap'n Redbeard of the good ship *Picaroon.*"

"This one thinks it a bad ship."

I gave him a pat on the shoulder. "Bright one! Funny Marmoona. Ye be a true jester indeed." What an effort I was making to keep nice with Marmoona, but just as an anchor is drawn to the ocean bottom, whenever I so much as glanced at the critter, me eyes were drawn straight down to the golden key. Of course I wanted the key back, Li'l Whisker, but if I demanded that Marmoona return it, he would certainly remind me of the home I had so thoroughly ravaged. I would try me best not to speak of the key. Don't be thinking I wouldn't get it back. It would be mine again for sure.

He stood a little taller on his knobby toes, looking off into the distance. As he gazed into the winding stalks, Marmoona was taken by a tremor of stillness. "This one must make a leave from here. Beardface should too."

With the force of his long legs, Marmoona launched from his position into a nearby clearing. An ominous sound spread over the island, seemingly creeping from the very ground where I stood. I whipped me head to the clearing only to catch Marmoona's shadow as it was yanked into a dense pocket of greenery. The creature offered one last piece of advice that floated on the wind kicking up behind his fleeing stride. "Shh! Shh is the only way to stay away from its minions when they come down! Fernobarb's minions hear the human pirate!" The speckle-belly disappeared inside the safety of the jungle's cover, leaving me kneeling 'tween the knotted roots of an enormous tree. I poked some caked dirt out of a section of the webbed roots, creating a perfect lookout, framed by twirling vines on the left and scalloped broad leaves on the right.

Me eyes were fixed on the ship and the shore where it lazed. The sun was just about to dig into the bronze waters. Under that cover I sat, wondering what I was hiding from. . . .

I heard them coming down the mountain, whizzing through the air along the rocky cliff as if they had fallen from the crystal peak. They were small black flying creatures, and when they weren't airborne they liked to jump great distances 'tween the rocks and tree trunks. Each of 'em looked to have three legs—two anchored in the back and one up front—and thar bodies were covered in a sleek stubbled shell that seemed as though it'd be hard to puncture. Alone, they didn't look like they were any match for

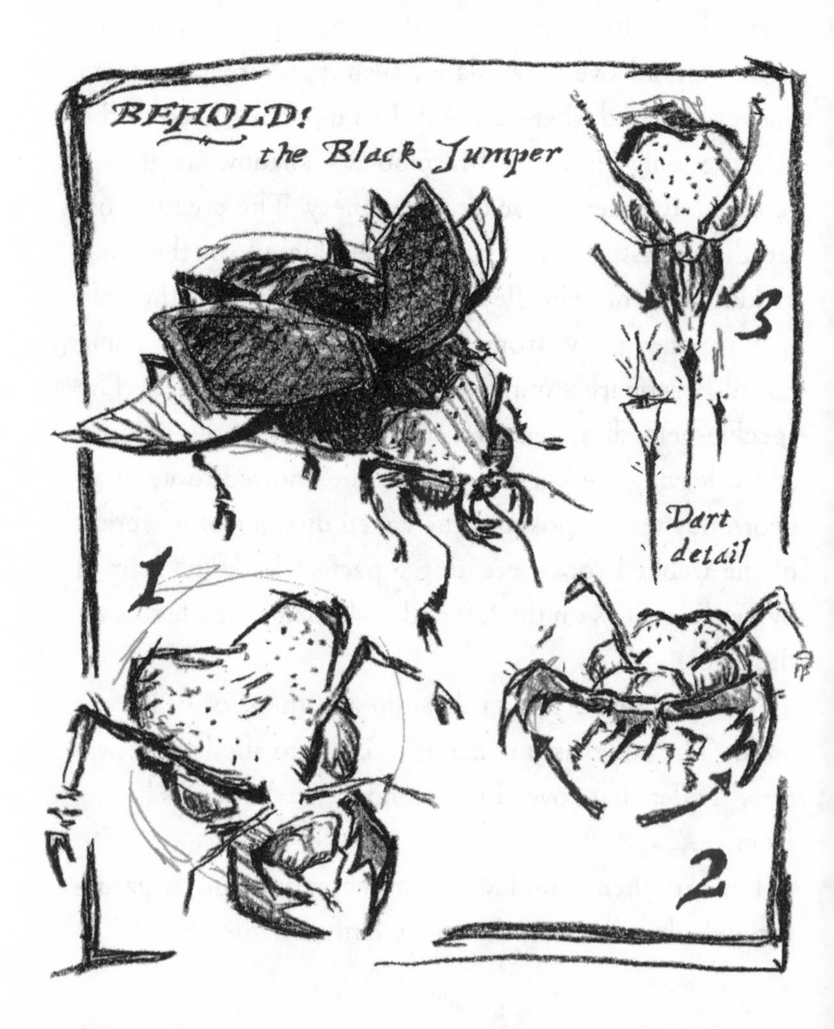

a real pirate, although they formed a fearsome bunch when grouped together, darting about with that horrible buzz they made when they flew. It made me ears wobble, and I didn't rightly appreciate that. I was ready to turn me back on 'em, as I've always made sure I pick fights only with those close to me own size, but I didn't get the chance to budge before the li'l black jumpers went flying right into the mighty *Picaroon*. Li'l Whisker, I wasn't looking for a fight, but I wasn't going to walk away while they had thar way with me own quarters. So I flew across the sand and quietly climbed aboard the ship, keeping me distance from the pests while I made out what they were up to down below.

When I heard the rasp from Jimmy's forgotten accordion, I knew the things had ventured at least as far as the crew's chambers. I followed thar ruckus and caught up with 'em in the galley. They seemed to be getting the lay of the land, like they were taking notes on all the glories of me ship so they could take 'em back to Fernobarb, thar no-good leader. I didn't want to waste any time letting 'em know who was captain of this ship. I grabbed a nearby shard of wood from where the base of the *Picaroon* had hit up against the shore. With the weapon clutched in me fist, I made me way toward the cluster, waiting for one of 'em minions to move so I could get a better angle. finally, I saw two of 'em veer off to the left, heading for the crew's chambers. So I raised the wood in me hand, and with me mangled teeth grinding against each other, I hurled the chunk toward the biggest jumper of 'em all. It struck him squarely on the side of his shell and he went tumbling to the deck. All the others shrieked with one giant buzz. I covered me ears before they fell off! A couple of 'em spied me in the corner, opening thar mouths and spewing bristly darts from tube tongues straight at me chest. The li'l hair-thin arrows didn't do any serious damage, but they did provide a good strong itch all the way down to me belly. Once they were satisfied with thar revenge, the black jumpers swooped down toward thar injured comrade and lifted him from the deck before droning past me, back out to safety. I chased 'em with me fist in the air and screamed as they flew across the beach: "Take that, ye no-good minions! Thar be more where that came from! And take the message back to yer no-good Fernobarb. Nobody messes with Cap'n Redbeard, and that includes no-good beasts! *And* their minions!" I watched 'em disappear round the coast.

Li'l Whisker, sometimes ye got to stand up for yerself, and here be a good example. I couldn't let 'em jumpers think they had the right to go stalking about on me own ship. I went down and did a quick pass through the *Picaroon* to make sure they hadn't caused her too much harm. To my surprise, the crew of jumpers had shown thar might in ransacking belowdecks. The door o' me cabin looked like it had been cracked by a joint and mighty force, but by the luck of a shooting starfish, nothing in me quarters had been harmed by the fiendish bunch. It would have been mighty powerful sad if me treasure trunk had been demolished. Why, I'd be telling a red-fisted lie if I said that the thought alone wouldn't squeeze a few drops from me eyes.

Across the cabin floor I moved, and as I did, I heard something rustling. I was certain I had chased every one of 'em minions away. It couldn't be one of 'em. And it was right near impossible for it to be Fernobarb, for, if those large footprints I traced up on the cliff were indeed his, he wouldn't be able to tuck himself away in a li'l corner.

Beneath me the wood bulged, rising and falling as if the *Picaroon* was gasping for air. Clearly something was down in the bilge, and it wanted out. Just shy of four paces I stood from the buckling boards, and as the force under them grew I increased the distance to seven. A plank snapped and sprang from the crossbeams, broadsiding me belly and knocking more than just the wind from me. I briefly stepped around the corner to the brig, where I could rub the pain from me aching tummy. As I leaned into the wall, a few more planks were popped from place. Thar echoes overlapped as they were tossed into a pile. I lined me face up with the corner and slowly edged me eye onto what was coming up from below.

Well, shiver me timbers, Li'l Whisker (and for once, I mean it literally), it weren't nothing more than a child climbing up from the busted floor. A child! Sweetening me voice, I took a step or two closer and announced me presence. "Hello thar."

The child shot from the hole and disappeared into the darkness farther down the hall.

"Me li'l one, are ye human?"

For a while thar was only the kid's breathing set to the pace of fear. Then the answer came. "Of course I'm human, you mean pirate, and I don't think it's a good idea to talk to you!" The mysterious girl's voice was young—strong, too.

She was a feisty one, to be sure. The li'l girl stayed in the dark, quiet, until a single hiccup stuttered out. Then another. The third hiccup waited a spell, and once it came it was chased by a hundred others.

"Make certain ye take a breath. Ye know, ye sound an awful lot like good Jimmy's accordion," I said. "Is thar somethin' I can do in the way o' helpin' ye?"

She answered with a simple hiccup.

"I must tell ye, dear, ye have me as curious as that fabled cat. For I thought I was the onliest person on this here island. Won't ye sharpen me up a bit and tell me where ye come from?"

She began to say something but held it before it escaped her lips.

"Please," I begged.

At long last she answered. "No"—*hiccup*—"I can't tell you. Do you know why?"

Me finger was pressed against me chin and I shook me

head. I guess thar was enough light for her to see me because she trumpeted, "Because, you big"—*hiccup*— "mean, forgetful pirate, if I told you"—*hiccup*—"I would be talking to you, and the last time I checked"—*hiccup*— "I'm still not talking to you."

"True enough, li'l lady, but ye've sunk me head in wonder. What if I ask ye one question, just one, and ye answer? Ye wouldn't so much be talkin' to me, just answerin' where I could hear ye, is all. How's that sit with ye?"

"I guess I can answer one question, but remember"—*hiccup*—"I'm not talking to you—just answering."

"Right ye are, lass. Just answerin', like I'm not even here. And on the certain matter of me one question, just how is it that a young girl comes to crawl up from the bilge o' me ship?"

"If you really want to know, I got here on my own. And then I had help from a pirate"—*hiccup*. "A helpful pirate. A nice pirate."

"Now, missy, don't be judgin' a book by its cover."

"Don't worry, I already know all about you, Redbeard. Every chapter of your story, backward and"—*hiccup*— "forward."

"Impossible!" I thundered.

"Possible!"

"How?" I stomped me foot. It was high time I demanded some answers.

"Not telling."

"Please."

"Nope."

I thought she was feisty before, but now she was proving to be downright ornery. "Well, yer lyin', then."

"No, I'm not."

"Yes, ye are—I know so!" I raised me finger toward the lass. Only as I did, I realized it didn't do much good, given how I couldn't see her and didn't know rightly where to point.

"How do you know I'm lying?"

" 'Cause thar ain't no such thing as a nice pirate . . . is thar?"

"Oh yes, there is, Redbeard, but you wouldn't know any of them since"—*hiccup*—"your crew up and left you."

"So ye knew me crew, did ye?"

"Oh yes, they were a colorful bunch." She hiccuped a bit o' bilge dust as she made the accusation.

"If I catch a hiccuping fit from one o' those hiccups o' yers, yer in for it!"

"You can't catch hiccups, Captain. I get them every"—*hiccup*—"now and again, when I'm scared."

I had to hand it to her, the little girl had a way for making words mean something. "Now look here, missy. I'm not that scary. I don't scare ye."

She and her hiccups paused as she thought. "But Redbeard, you do scare me. You even scared your crew so bad, they ran off."

"Now look here, li'l lady. I did no such thing. And

back to the point of me crew. How'd ye know they left?" I took a step toward the darkness where she was hiding.

"Well, I haven't seen them around—have you?"

"Wait a blasted minute, just how long've ye been down there in the bilge?"

"As long as you've been lost at sea"—*hiccup*—"Redbeard. No map, no sail, then the helm—unbelievable."

"Impossible!"

"Possible!"

"But when did ye come aboard?"

"Not so fast, Redbeard. I answered your one question"—*hiccup*—"so as far as I'm concerned, we're back to not talking."

"Fine, fine." I tipped me hat, trying to show a bit o' politeness. "Then just give me yer name, li'l miss, and we'll be done with this un-conversation before it even starts."

"No, Redbeard. I'm not answering any of your questions, and I'm sure as day not going to tell you my name."

"I'll tell ye me name."

"I already know it."

"No, ye don't—not me real name."

"Ferdinand Igneominious."

"Impossible!"

"Possible!"

"How do ye know that?"

"If I've told you once, I've told you a thousand times—no questions."

"That may be what ye said, but unfortunately for ye, ye are now bound to answer one question since ye didn't give me yer name."

"Says who?"

"Says me. It's a new rule of the *Picaroon*." She had played me long enough, Li'l Whisker. Now I needed to take charge. "Any person withholdin' her name must release the answer to a question o' the captain's choosin'."

I could hear the li'l miss grumbling in the shadows. "Fine, Redbeard, I'll play by your no-good rules."

I straightened me back and cleared me throat. "Now then, tell me exactly how ye got on the ship and how ye've managed to stay alive."

"No fair!"

"What do ye mean? Ye said I could ask one more question."

"No, I didn't. You told me I had to answer one more question. And besides, that wasn't a question. It was a command. Don't you know anything, Redbeard?"

"Right ye are, miss. Let me put it another way: will ye now be so kind as to tell me how ye came to board the *Picaroon* and how ye've survived fer so long?"

"That's two questions."

"Aye, I knew ye'd be makin' such a claim, but in truth it's just one humble question split into two equal parts."

"Fine, Your Highness Captain." She blubbered her lips. "I'll tell the whole story just so you can get your way. I hope you're happy."

"Aye, I am indeed."

"As I was saying, here's how it happened. It wasn't the *Picaroon* that found me. I found the *Picaroon.*"

"How?"

"When you had her docked at Blackpool, my hometown. I knew it was time for me to set sail in search of adventure, so I spent the better part of six days studying each and every ship, watching the crews, seeing which vessel it was that was calling me."

"And the *Picaroon,* she spoke the loudest, did she?"

"No, Redbeard, it was your crew that caught my eye. They worked together and stuck together and I could tell it was a good bunch. So when Jonah took the rowboat out in the early hours of the morning to do some fishing, I knew it was my best chance. As he drifted closer to the docks, I dipped into the water quietly and went out to meet the dinghy. It was while he was wrestling with a giant lobster that I leapt in and hid in the bait trough without him ever knowing I was there."

"Did ye say he was wrestlin' a giant lobster?" I couldn't help letting a tiny grin creep its way onto me face at the thought.

"It was for your birthday—I know, I know, Redbeard. Jonah told me all about the tradition."

"When did he tell ye?"

"When he found me that evening hiding in his stove. It was a good spot, I fit just perfect, only it wasn't the safest place to be. Boy, let me tell you, Jonah let out the biggest scream you've ever heard when he saw me in there. Dr. Pauley Wog was there too, so he came over and met me."

"And just what was the good doctor doin' in the galley during office hours?"

"He was peeling potatoes!"

"Oh, yes, of course."

"And why do you make the doctor peel the potatoes?"

"It's simple, missy. Thar be not enough work of the medical variety to keep him busy on the *Picaroon.*"

"That's because you wouldn't let Porthole Pete get his leg wrapped up when it was cut, or give Maximilian any relief for his aching muscles."

"They knew the rules. No seein' the doctor unless I approve. Thar be no room fer sissies aboard the *Picaroon.* And a three-inch gash across the calf don't rightly count as a legitimate injury. Besides, the good doctor's quite handy with a peeler. But I wouldn't let him be workin' down thar in the lap o' luxury if I knew he'd be talkin' to a no-good stowaway like yerself. What'd he say to ye?"

"He asked me all kinds of questions about where I'd come from and said that I couldn't be half bad if I managed to sneak by everyone like I had. He and Jonah promised they'd take care of me, and above all, they promised they'd protect me from their awful captain."

"They didn't say that. Yer lyin', fluffin' that part up so yer story sounds better."

"They did say it. So did your whole crew. You should've

spent a few nights down there yourself, eavesdropping in the galley. You could have learned a lot."

"Well, how do ye know ole Jonah wasn't lyin' about me?"

"Because, Redbeard, he disappeared into the ocean when you kicked him out from under you. I think that's a sure sign that he was telling the truth."

"How do ye know about that?"

"Your whole crew saw it. Dr. Pauley Wog told me. He said it had become too dangerous for me to stay and he planned on letting me out in the next town where you docked. That's when he moved me to the bilge, where he stored his extra food."

"Extra food?"

"You always took more than your fair share, Redbeard."

"Aye, so I've been told."

"The only problem was, Dr. Pauley Wog forgot to wake me up when they all jumped ship."

I couldn't help letting out a hearty chuckle. "Aye, he forgot about the li'l stowaway, did he?"

"That's stove-away, Redbeard. Can't you catch on to anything?"

"I'm afraid ye better check with yer dictionary back home, li'l missy—"

"I don't need to check anything, Redbeard. I know what a stove-away is. It's what Dr. Pauley Wog and Jonah called me, and they explained what it meant, so I don't need any more help. Now, that's all I have to tell you, so I'm done talking. If you would be so kind as to clear out so I can exit without having to look at your evil face, I would like it just fine."

At that, she dashed toward me, rubbing her eyes with her li'l hands. Before I could reach for her, she jumped through me hands, stomping on me bootless toes with both feet. Just before she ran out of sight, she hunkered down and spit on the crown of me only remaining boot. I barely caught a glimpse of the yellow curls falling over the back o' her overalls. She didn't bother looking back as I yelled after her: "Fair enough. If ye wants to play that way, then fend for yerself. Ye can be Fernobarb's guest!"

I went up on deck and the bright sun fell through the rigging, casting a warm shadow net over me skin. When I made me way back to the stern of the ship, I looked down at the water lapping up against the crashed *Picaroon.* I wasted no time striking me colors until I was standing thar in me crossboned long johns. A quick count o' three and a pinch of the nose later, I was breaking down below the cool turquoise surface.

It woke me up, paddling across the waves. Deep in the clear water I spied a whole mess of goodies—yellow coral, purple pearls, and a giant octopus that looked frightening until he turned around and showed me that clown face of his. I did a few frog stroke laps 'tween the *Picaroon* and a nearby tangle of dancing seaweed. At the floor of the ocean I found a clamshell that weren't like any I've ever seen, for it was shaped like a triangle and was big enough to take up me whole hand. Once at the surface, I scooped water into the shell and slowly poured its stream over me head. Floating on me back, I stared up into the distance at the crystal peak of the Fundorado mountaintop and, just below, the cave that split the giant waterfall into two streams, spraying down either side of the gaping hole. With all the exploring this island was begging me to do, I knew thar weren't no time to keep a watch on me treasure chest. Me mission was clearer than the waters of Spangled Beach: I had to lug me heavy load up the mountainside and bury it, safe and sound, in that cave. And while I was at it, I might as well be on the lookout for a new home. With the *Picaroon* out of commission, and me cabin cold and drafty, I'd have to find a new place to lay me tired head at night. It wouldn't be easy finding a spot up to me strict standards—especially on land, seeing how I'd much rather be sleeping at sea. But if any place could provide me with a top-notch sleeping spot with all the comforts of the big blue, it was certainly Fundorado Island.

The peak disappeared behind the veils of ocean spray kicked up by me feet. For the first time in a stone's age I was relaxed. The sun drenched me belly and I drifted, ever so lazily, in circles toward the ship. On me knees, I took a handful o' the sea 'n' smacked it to me face like a Nipponese tidal wave. I tossed me hair to 'n' fro, whipping the wayward droplets from its flying strands. I rose to me feet and leaned against the *Picaroon*'s sideboards as I tiptoed out o' the water.

After a drying-out nap under the edge of the jungle, I wrung a few squirts o' juice from a plump piece of spongefruit. Thinking about that girl drove me batty; I hadn't had a stowaway in over twenty-some-odd years. That li'l missy must have had a capital setup down in the bilge. I went over to have a quick look-see. 'Fore I knew it, I was crawling into her li'l hiding spot. As I crouched below the buckled boards, the light spilled in through the deck overhead, lighting me damp and cold passageway. I crawled farther along, and me face met up squarely with an abandoned spiderweb stretched from side to side. I pushed back, pulling the stringy bits out from between the black hairs of me red beard.

When I rested me husky hand against the slimy wall of the bilge, I felt the pitter-patter of little claws scurrying across me forearm. When I looked down I saw a rat resting on me skin. It weren't till it scooted forward, highlighting its tail in the single beam of light managing to get all the way down thar, that I realized this was Juliet, Googler's ole pet rat. This weren't just any rat. Juliet had the longest tail of them all, so long that Googler had to care for her by braiding it into a fine knot, the only knot that would hold the thing out of the way. We called it a lover's hitch, as it was a product of Googler's own invention. Li'l Juliet scrambled by me, 'n' 'fore I knew it, she had crawled her way up and out of the bilge. I carried on, inching forward to the small spot of ship where the young miss had apparently been laying her head every night. It was thar that I found an envelope tucked away under her small pillow. I also found a couple o' empty pouches o' ship biscuits, and, lucky for me, a few that were still half full. The li'l lady had been eating like a queen the whole time while I was starving out at sea with those no-good jelly beans. But at least I now had a hearty snack to put away as I opened up the letter and read what had been written:

To Penny, My Dear Tuppence,

I am afraid I have some terrible news. The crew has collectively decided to abandon this ship. Captain Redbeard has, for too long now, gotten away with the most egregious acts as leader of a noble crew. You should have heard the pure hysterics that poured out of that grown man's mouth when he saw what was in those barrels. I had been told and now I believe it: the man does not like jelly beans!

On a personal note, Googler let it spill that I am indeed not a real pirate, but a forty-year-old doctor who has fled his practice and home to seek out a different life, which has, obviously, not turned out quite the way I had hoped. I do not regret my little adventure, as it has brought me many life lessons. Although I do regret trying to fool these rogues into believing that I had some variation of an ancient war wound under this silly patch over my eye. (I'll let you in on my little secret,

(Dear Penny; as Googler now knows, I am sure this information will spread halfway to China by nightfall: I do not, in reality, need the patch. My eyes are both in quite good shape. Do you know how hard it is to feign medium-range blurriness when you have been blessed with perfect vision? I guess this also means that Maximilian will now know that I did in fact see those aces.)

I thank you for all the nights you lent me your generous ear. It felt good getting all this so-called soul seasickness off my chest.

Unfortunately for me, I will not be able to enjoy your company any longer, for I have been informed that you will not be joining us for our reverse mutiny. There is adequate reason. First and foremost, between you and me, I don't think McGee has a clue what he's doing. This journey is going to be a treacherous and largely improvised one, as we do not have an agreed-upon destination, nor do we have accurate coordinates for our present location. (Redbeard has never been known for fastidious record-keeping, and the penmanship was, well, a bit smudged.) From what we can tell, we are at least two and a half days from the coast of China. It wouldn't be right, exposing you to an escape with such minuscule chances for survival. Honestly, I would prefer to not expose myself to this either, but then again, I have sort of backed myself into a corner here, haven't I? Damn that blood oath! But we did want you to know that we love you, Penny. I for one greatly admire your pluck. I think you are an exceptional young lady, and I do think that one day you will have a blue jay, that beautiful bird you have so longed to have sing to you at night. I also recognize that you are on your own now, an orphan of the sea, and we do not want to leave you without making some arrangements for your escape. So please do read carefully: once Redbeard wakes up, he will be in quite a huff. As you have done so wisely for the last several weeks, steer clear of him. He will unleash an unbearable cacophony of aggression when he sees that we've left all the barrels for him. If we know anything, we know that he will turn this ship southward and head to Madagascar for yet another crew. Being a man of great tradition, he will dock at the far end of the harbor. There you will find a cluster of rocks on the starboard side (that's the right to you and me—I could never keep those things straight in my head). Jump down and climb across until you are safely on land. Fifty paces to your right (Mort insists it is more like seventy, but we all know he has a short stride), you will find an unassuming alleyway. Follow it until it dead-ends at the doorstep of a tavern. Run around to the back and look for a small door hidden behind a broken carriage. Knock on that door four times. Only four times, Penny. A very generous, albeit forcefully so, woman will answer. Her name is Ma Carruthers. She is an old friend of Billy Bilgewater. (She designed but did not implement the vile tattoo on his left arm.) Tell her you know Billy, tell her your story and she will look after you.

Adieu, young Penny. I will miss you. And if the stars align, perhaps our paths will cross again one day.

Yours,

Dr. Pauley Wog

P.S. Googler has a small request to make, so I will now pass the note off to him. . . .

Hiya Penny,

Maybe ye know who is writing this. I am Googler writing right now! Dr. Pauley Wog let me tell ye some things 'cause I will miss ye. I want ye to look after Juliet, me rat. Like I told ye, she's named after me only true love, so ye can guess how much she means to me. She has a like for ye better than any of the other crew. Ye are brave. I will miss ye, Penny!

Yer Googler

Penny,

Ye might not know who this is but ye will once ye get to the bottom of the letter and feast yer eyes on me signature. I'm not quite sure I have anything to tell ye but it was drivin' me crazy the whole time when they wouldn't let me hold the pen. I hope ye don't mind, but I fished the letter out from the crack in the floor where the doctor and Googler left it. I did so with the sole intention of openin' up yer envelope here and makin' sure me voice was heard. Ye are me favorite Penny of all time. Even if I meet another one, I'll always let it be known that ye were the best and luckiest.

And now I sign off,

Maximilian, Tiger of Trinidad

Mort

I don't know about ye, Li'l Whisker, but for me this letter answered a lot of questions! For starters, it confirmed me hunch that the li'l lady couldn't rightly have survived on her own. Me no-good crew was helping her out when they should've been manning the ship. I can't explain it, but looking at that letter, I somehow knew it had already been read a hundred times. Thar even looked to be a cluster of tearstains splattered across Maximilian's oversized signature. Googler must've been in some state to leave his beloved behind on the ship. I figured it only right to seek her out before heading back to me chambers. Juliet didn't have a chance of lasting a day on Fundorado with those minions and the like. Neither did the li'l lady named Penny, but thar weren't much I could do to help her if she insisted on bruising me boot and running off with that stubbornness of hers.

Finding the rodent proved to be easier than I thought it'd be. For when I stepped back out onto Spangled Beach, I saw her timidly pressed up against the damp wood of the *Picaroon.* Seeing the way she trembled, I knew she wouldn't put up much of a fight if I tried to rein her in. So I took off me hat and slowly bent down before I snatched her up into it and carried her off to me chambers. I didn't rightly know how to keep her from running off in the middle of the night, so I made a sleeping sack out of me stocking to slip her into. It weren't too easy grabbing her in me hand, for her coat was nice and slick. Even when I did get her stashed away, she rolled back and forth inside the fabric. The only way to be sure she stayed in place was by securing the stocking deep inside me only remaining boot, which I removed and placed next to me chest. With me hammock not surviving the crash, I didn't have any place to prop me feet up, so I curled up tighter than a conch shell on the treasure and tried to get some shuteye.

Day 3

Thar weren't much sleep to be had that night. Or more to the point, what li'l of it thar was, I just couldn't seem to get to it, 'tween Juliet, me broken hammock and the sand's spookish orange glow creeping through me window. It's no surprise that I raised the white flag and gave up on me shuteye. It was still dark outside. Had it not been for the stardust shore's warm honey light, I wouldn't have been able to see a solitary thing. I chipped what little sleep there was from me eyes 'n' crawled over me boot to wake Juliet. But, Li'l Whisker, Juliet was more than asleep. In a flurry, I tugged the fat black stocking from me shoe and rolled the end down around her head. Maybe she needed water or a crumbling corner of toast. Maybe all she needed was some fresh air. Me boots can have a tangy way of offending innocent noses. Whatever she needed, I couldn't give it to her any longer, for Juliet the rat was no more. I pressed her pudgy tummy to me ear and searched for a trace of hope, but thar was nothing. The li'l dose of tragedy would probably be a bit too much for Penny to take, so I figured it might be best to work out the proper words 'fore I spoke 'em to her. With any luck, I would have some comfortable tidings for her the next time we happened upon each other.

Me jump from the railing squeezed a faint li'l flash from the sand beneath me feet. Through the hard carved shadows of the shore I stumbled till the dark morning surf gathered around the toes of me bootless foot.

I hoisted Juliet high in me hand just under the lacey thin silver of the moon. For a moment or two, I held her up thar, trying to get some light to shine off those faraway eyes. With me fingers rooting deep in the curls of me beard, I broke the cool silence with a few words for the former rat. "Juliet, bein' a rat can't be an easy thing. Most folks want to smother ye with the tufts o' thar brooms 'n' fling ye down the coal hole. Ye ought to be glad Googler saw ye for more than a filthy rodent. Ye got true stars overhead for that, ye know. When yer in need of someone else to take care of ye"—I knelt in the sand—"and this lesson might be for the both of us—everyone ain't cut out for takin' care of others." She rolled from me palm to the slick, glittering surface. A gentle fold of surf swept up, clung to Juliet snug in the stocking and rushed her out past the restless breakers. "The tides know yer course," I cried out before turning to make me way up the boulders beyond the *Picaroon*.

At the ledge of a great plateau, I stood tall over the ship and the sea that brought me here. The sun began its trek over the island with a li'l ray of light, peeking from the ocean's curve in the east. Again, I turned and stared across to the expansive field's far end. It was a flat stretch of wild grass, rising high above the surrounding area. Beyond the plateau, a mountain range pinched into a long, notched fin and ran (from what I could gather) south down the center length of the island. The jagged mountain face came into focus as I strolled through the paling gray morning. Me path was littered with pitted stones, so I took gingerly steps for me denuded foot. From the chalky sky, a sunbeam fell; then (as tends to happen) more came to join in. I sank me hands into me pockets and felt the toasty rays play upon me shoulders.

The Fundorado sun has a mighty curious effect on some of the rocks of the land. After thar touched by the light, those pitted stones quiver about in the most indescribable fashion. Even 'fore I had time to be alarmed, five or six of the fist-sized rocks popped up in high arcs. *Clunk! Clunk! Splash!* They landed in the heavy grass and puddles. The field was in bedlam. Hop rocks rained down, slugging hard on me back, shoulders and kneecaps. Some o' them stones were angry. One o' the more serious blows took an earring out 'n' had me sharp teeth cutting me mouth up in a blinding flinch. The air was so clouded by rocks, it made no difference that I dropped me hat down to me brow 'n' gamboled round the tough sluggers with me eyes closed.

Like an anchor, I fell fast and straight. Me aimless running launched me right over the plateau's sudden break. I flailed about, all but cartwheeling down the unforgiving slope. The landing crunched me poor body through a tight ring of branches. In the moments before I realized I was going to be trapped, I took note of the peculiar plant formation surrounding me. Its shape was borrowed from a bulb of garlic; it domed out at the base and came to a scraggly point at the top. Morning dew ran along the outside branches and dribbled on me as I crouched in the center. The hop rocks were still quite jumpy, leaping from the ledge on high to the resilient branches of me shelter. I was on a riverbank—a riverbank swelling like a bloated sow. The river's edge gnawed away at the bush's grip of the soil, and on the other side, stones beat against it, snapping it from its hold.

Into the rush of water we went: me, the pen of branches, even the close circle of earth it was rooted to . . . everything jarred from the bank and was tearing over the flow. Thankfully, the tumble tree had, by nature, the fight to stay afloat and upright. The spindly branches, however, were another story. They did absolutely no good in keeping the headwater off me. The sun shone over a harmless pink line of clouds. The river widened up a bit 'n' flowed on a more soothing current. As Fundorado Island's scenery moved by, I wanted to leap from me cage and touch all the unimaginable sights I was seeing.

This here's me
tumble tree 'n'
a rubbing taken
from the ruins.

When the tumble tree bobbed around in an open marsh, I stood and popped me head through two o' the branches. With me hat, I fanned a look of disbelief from me face. That disbelief was for the family o' miniature horses gathered by the shady reeds of the water's edge. The horses were, oh, I'd say not much more than a boot tall, and they came in all sorts of colors: amber, ebony, jade—and even a few piebalds. They were right in front of me, the lot of 'em, napping and playing away in the manner horses do best. A fearless li'l white one paddled out toward the tumble tree. I stretched me arm as far as I could and tickled the water's rippled surface. "And what a wonder ye are, tiny fella. I doubt the world's ever seen a more delightful creature."

Afloat in the water, he gave a whisper-thin neigh. Through me nose, I responded with a singsong sigh, but it didn't match his tune. I reached into me front pocket and broke off a chunk o' ship biscuit for him. From the gap in the branches, I tossed the morsel his way. The flaky piece looked like a wedding cake next to the li'l scamp. His tiny mouth locked down tight on a corner. He tilted his head back and took quick bites at it from the bottom up. The rest of the herd rushed toward him, curious for thar own taste o' the ship biscuit, no doubt. Thar charge set the still water in motion, pushing me back out to the pull of the river. I drifted under a dense cover of trees before I could see him eat the whole thing.

Among the trees, the river became shallow and its pace deadened to a sliding slumber. The tumble tree twirled in a slow spiral. Every breath I drew became sticky from the steam caught between the twisting trunks. All the smoky haze made it tough, but I was able to spot some movement behind an ashy pocket of trees. The river slowly pulled me deeper into the thicket. First I recognized the bent staff, for it disagreed with the natural lines of the sparse forest. Then its owner, ever so distant in the wood, stepped forward. It was the no-good key thief, Marmoona! And slinking in his blurry wake was the feline creature, no doubt, for I heard him calling after it, "Whip Cat comes to this one!" The cat listened with scooped ear and its creepy hooked tail sway-hanging overhead. It looked like Marmoona was drawing a line on the ground with his staff. He reached into a sack tied to his stick and scattered a handful of seeds in the split mud. He continued to carve the land farther, and each time sprinkled it in the same manner. What in heaven was that confounded critter planting?

Me ears hunted for sounds, and they were few. A cast o' drumbugs thumping in slow rolling waves, the sound of the thin twigs of the tumble tree rattling against the breeze—I heard 'em sure enough. But I also heard the sound of a good idea hatching in me head. If the specklebelly hadn't seen me yet, I could slip out o' the boat and sneak me way up to him and, more importantly, to me key. That was all the thought I needed 'fore me hands were around the branches, trembling to get 'em apart. I fought hard, prying away at different sets of sticks. Don't be thinking these bushes were stone-pillar strong or me arms granny-knot weak. I moved the greenery plenty, just not enough to fit through.

At a fair-sized pool, the river quickened again. The tumble tree spun with the current, but I crept around inside to keep Marmoona in sight. For some time, the current steadily increased, racing along at a solid clip. The speckle-belly got the urge to alter his speed, for he and the Whip Cat were keeping pace with me far off in the timber-spotted mist. The water gradually cut lower into the ground until I had to crane me neck to see the base o' the trees. Practically roaring now, the river frothed 'tween tight canyon walls as it slid farther 'n' farther underground. The tall, narrow canyon sealed up at the top, and I found meself not just alone in a wooden cage-bush, but also trapped on the water in a dark tunnel. I continued moving in the blackness with the tumble tree grinding into the rocks as the river dragged me farther. I could feel wet clouds of steam against me face. Its vapors sizzled upon me lips 'n' stung the pink corners of me eyes. Finally, the dark gave way and the tunnel opened up to a towering thin shaft. Sunlight snuck past the thick white curls of steam to highlight the discolored surface of the circular stone chamber. In the light I saw that several river tunnels joined here, something like the spokes meeting at the center of a ship's wheel.

The tumble tree knocked to a stop at the foot of the shaft. Beneath the raft's earthen base the colliding rivers turned livid, hissing 'n' bubbling. Boiling coils of water erupted from the tiny space 'tween the raft's hardened, muddy root base and the long stretch up to the top. I coughed out a heavy plume of steam and grabbed a branch to steady meself from a sudden tipping. At the high end of the base a wide sheet of steam shot along the chamber wall. I stumbled to the side, leveling off the tumble tree.

At this leveling-off, the whole raft shinnied just a bit up the shaft. Steam was expanding with such great force under me, it was actually lifting the tumble tree. Thar I sat, crouched in the middle of it all, as the raft jolted in sputtering jerks. I fell to the clumpy floor with me face pressed into the dirt and embedded pebbles. In a thundering burst, the tumble tree exploded up the chamber, screaming out the opening of a great mound of earth. Following the airborne raft, a lush layer o' steam spilled forth and inked its way around the lofty peak. Having reached the top of me blast, I landed hard on the ring o' steam and rode it as a cushion for most of the turbulent way down. A stout shrub snagged the bottom and set the tumble tree a-tumbling. I crunched into the branches over 'n' over as we toppled. A great crack signaled the end of me journey. The raft was caved in on one side. Pieces of the tumble tree went adrift in one of the rivers that looked like it would feed back to the steam shaft.

"This one . . . this one maybe will never stop laughing."

Me head was wedged under a broken branch, so all I saw were Marmoona's two flat yellow feet striding from the brush as he said this. "When Beardface shot in the air, this one got funny smiles." The speckle-belly stuck his hand in and helped me from the splintered pile o' wood. "When is funny one to do it again?"

"What?" I asked, scraping a few pebbles from me whiskers.

"When to fly from the mountain?"

I fixed me eye on the strand around his neck and me key's sweet shine. "If ye got such a jolly good time out of it, maybe I'll have to show ye meself one day."

The Whip Cat leapt from a vine to the tumble tree's scattered ribs. He sat thar batting away at a feather stuck to his mouth, and when his face was clean, he broke into a sprint, then trailed just behind us the rest o' the way through the woods.

Upon me arrival at the *Picaroon,* I found Penny on her hands and knees, circling the deck underneath Marmoona's fallen tree. "What in the name o' Davey Jones are ye up to?"

"Good day. I'm doing something on my own, if you don't mind."

"Well, what is it yer doin', so I'll know how to stay out o' yer way?"

"I can't find my rat."

I snagged me foot a li'l on the frayed planks from the

shipwreck. How could I have forgotten about Juliet? All this time and I hadn't remembered to come up with the right words for Penny. I joined the poor girl out on the deck, ducking under the fruit-filled tangle. The truth could rest till I figured how to say it.

I scooted a barrel out from the railing and pretended to look for a rat that just plain wasn't thar. "How long have ye been pokin' round for it?" I asked.

"Maybe all the way from morning," she mumbled, with her head underneath a cannon housing. "I'm sorry for going through your stuff. I only looked where I thought Juliet might be hiding."

She was good at making a fella feel bad. With a sorry hand on her shoulder, I let just a wink o' guilt out into the open. "Now, it's probably me turn to look for Googler's rat. Ye best have a walk and go play."

"Juliet belongs to me," Penny grumbled. "I'll stop when I find her."

I went over to her side of the ship 'n' hung me beard over her dirty face. "When it's me time to look, I won't stop until I find Juliet either. Now ye get some rest so ye'll be fresh as a daisy when me turn is over." Up the port companionway I climbed, peeping under each step and finding hidden crannies I had never seen. Penny watched me investigate the ship, then hopped off and disappeared around the outcropping of rocks.

Not much later I was lying under the smashed tree thinking about me situation. A gimlet shriek broke me concentration. The mound of cinnamon fruits I piled on me chest scattered as I tracked the noise beyond the great boulders. "Penny!" I hollered again and again. "Penny!" I dropped to a li'l lip of shore and traced a path along a guarded alcove that tucked back into a sandy-bottomed cave. The li'l girl's head was buried in the rock. Her hands were cupped to the sides of her face to hide her frightened brown eyes. Across from us was a breathtaking sight to be sure—it even gave me a bit o' the willies. Caught in the pointed fingers of stone, a yellow skeleton was splayed out. Pouring off the skull and twining down an outstretched arm, locks of gritty, brittle hair playfully caught the briny gusts funneling through the cave. Below a set of peeling ribs, the spine continued, but not in human form. The backbone extended farther down than the feet would have been, ending at the remains of a crescent tail. A fish tail, Li'l Whisker! What me eyes were seeing could not be disputed. "It's only a skeleton, just a mermaid skeleton. Nothin' at all to be feared of." I crouched in the damp sand and unwound a curl of scarlet hair from the delicate ivory fingers. A crystal ring hooped loosely around the pinky, where thar was so much less to cling to than thar used to be.

Down its arm I drew me finger, collecting black dust and green growth from ages gone by. The fin had dried tough, and its prickles tickled me palm. I noticed bones scattered in the dark reaches of the cave, and pieces of other skeletons lying about.

"I'm not afraid, Redbeard." She leaned in closer for a better look. "It's only that I didn't know a skeleton would be here. That's why I screamed. I wasn't scared." She stood behind me 'n' leaned forward to get a touch of the thing. Her grime-lined fingernails stroked the needle-like spines of the tail, tinkering out a hollow note for every bone. "What did she look like when she was alive, I wonder." The ancient carcass sat motionless as Penny braved an eye-to-eyehole look inside the smiling skull.

"Well, for one thing, I can't imagine she'd be anythin' but a vision."

"Eww! It's not pretty in there!" Penny said as she pulled her head away.

"Har-har!" I roared. "Good to see yer not scared."

"I'm not scared anymore. I think it's positively stupendous. A real live mermaid right in front of me."

"She's not so live anymore," I said, chuckling. "So you believe in mermaids, do ye?"

"Why not? There's one right here in front of us." Her eyes found the sparkle of the crystal ring. Silently, she slipped it off and pressed the treasure down into her pocket. "I have a question." Her finger waved at me as she continued. "When you came running after me, you were calling out my name, no?"

"Yes."

"Well, how do you know my name?"

"Miss Girlie, it just so happens that I found a li'l note o' yers from Dr. Pauley Wog and Googler."

"And Maximilian."

"And Maximilian. And the paper clearly had yer name on it. Besides, ye already knew me name. Why, ye could whisper it to a friend and that friend to a few more and soon I could go deaf from the roar."

On a streaked rock she took a seat next to the mermaid.

"And what a fine name indeed, Penny! How smart! No wonder the *Picaroon* weathered such rough seas. A storm's a breeze when ye have a lucky penny tucked in yer bilge."

Penny raised her head. "Do you really think I'm lucky?"

"To be sure, somethin' kept the ship afloat, somethin' lucky. I can't see why it couldn't've been ye."

She swept her hair behind her ears and cupped her hands round her mouth. "Because I'm the most unluckiest girl in the world! All I wanted was an adventure and I got stuck with the meanest, most rotten-cored pirate who ever lived."

If what she said was true I wouldn't have felt so bad hearing it. "Oh, me dear Penny, that just be what I wanted people to think. I'm only half bad. Look down at the skeleton—"

"The mermaid?"

"Aye, the mermaid. Doubtful ye've ever seen anythin' like that before. This here Fundorado Island is full o' surprises. Ye came seekin' adventure? Well, pickin' the

Picaroon was an awfully smart choice, 'cause look where she landed ye—right in the lap o' legend! Ye've got yerself an ingenious eye for excitement. Ye weren't unlucky at all. It was a wise move o' yers to stow away." As I spoke, she surveyed the pounding waves beyond the cave and understood that it truly was something ripped from a fancy book.

"Hmm . . ." She thought out loud. "The trip hiding from you on the ship was fairly terrible, but this island does have a lot to be explored. I guess it was a wise choice. You're right, Redbeard, this will turn out to be a fine adventure."

"Dearie, ye can't go and pick yer favorite parts and pieces. The journey started long ago—yer adventure's already begun."

Penny dug her hand into her pocket and I could see her li'l fist wrapped around the crystal ring. "It can't *all* be my adventure. A little bit of it must be yours."

"Aye, aye, Lucky Penny. Truer words have ne'er been spoken."

We walked out of the cave together. I helped her up some of the boulders and was pleasantly surprised when at a few of the larger ones she needed no assistance at all. Every nook she passed was roughly inspected. "Do you think Juliet wandered from the *Picaroon*?"

Careful to keep me answer as honest as possible, I spoke. "Li'l Penny, I don't think Juliet is still roamin' round the ship. I'm sure she's moved on somewhere else."

Penny looked in the greenery and glanced round her feet. "That means she could be anywhere on this giant island. Can you help me, Redbeard?"

"Yer going to hunt through every belt o' jungle? In the wet pits of all those caves? And what about the canyons and mountains? Ye'll scour every corner o' Fundorado for a li'l rat?"

"That's right, Redbeard." She gave me a look of sincerity. "Please help!"

"O' course, Lucky Penny. I'll lend ye a hand." Penny had no idea that Juliet was long gone, and it was evident by the way she looked for her. I stuck me head in the trunks o' dead trees and crawled about in sticky thickets. But, Li'l Whisker, ye already know I didn't find a thing. It got so late I couldn't hold me eyes open any longer. I tried to convince the young lady to finish searching in the morning. But she refused.

"Redbeard, if you were lost, would you want somebody to wait until morning?"

I boomed out, "I'm a captain, not a rat!"

Penny's face got red. She moved away in a huff, and when I could see her no more she screamed: "And I'm not color-blind! At least Juliet has someone who cares for her, Blackbeard!"

Blackbeard . . . as if I hadn't heard that one before.

Day 4

The next morning I still had that li'l sassy Penny on me mind. I couldn't shake her. Not only was she sure to meet her doom whenever Fernobarb or his minions decided to get their hands on her, but she would also probably prove to be a nuisance as I tried to settle in on Fundorado. I don't work so well with landlubbers or li'l know-it-all scoundrels who like to get in me way. It seemed certain that before I could get me treasure to a new and improved hiding spot and before I could find a new abode for meself, I'd have to find a way to get young Penny off the island, out of harm's way and out of me own way.

Li'l Whisker, one of the first secrets to being a true adventurer, whether yer on land or at sea, is knowing how to make the most of the goods ye've been given. Lucky for me, I was living on a piece of land that didn't seem to have much in the way of limits where useful wonders were concerned. If I wanted to get that li'l miss off the island, then me starting point was obvious: I needed to get me hands on one of 'em tumble trees and fashion it into a raft she could use for safe sailing. And from thar her fate would be in the hands of the wind. Maybe she'd even be guided by a Great-Grandpa Gust, and if so, she'd pick her own price to pay.

I could trace me steps back to the tumble trees. I could even gather the parts for turning one of 'em into a reliable seafaring vessel, but I couldn't take one more step off the *Picaroon* without first finding a way to make sure me beloved treasure was guarded.

Seeing how I was without a crew, it seemed that me only option was to enlist the services of Penny. Of course, I didn't trust her, so I couldn't rightly track her down and spell out the help I was needing in plain language. I'd have to give the duty a spin, tell her that her expertise was needed to protect the mighty *Picaroon.* While she stood there, keeping a youthful eye on me ship, she'd also be watching after me chest without knowing it. Li'l Whisker, it was me best and only choice.

I knew it wouldn't be too hard to find the li'l lady, for she probably hadn't explored the terrain like I had been doing for the last few days. And she didn't know the first thing about fending for herself, seeing how Dr. Pauley Wog gave her everything without making her ask. So I figured she had run off near the base of the broken tree, somewhere over by the rocky patch Marmoona was claiming as his home. Ye can imagine how surprised I was to find that she had made it over to the entrance of the Jumbled Jungle. I caught her just as she was about to plunge deep into the greenery.

"Hold it right there, Penny."

She jumped back with a hiccup. I figured I should try to sweeten the conversation by removing me hat. But that didn't seem to mean much to her, for no sooner did she see me than she grabbed hold of the nearest tree and climbed her way up to the first sturdy branch she could find, just out of arm's reach. I made me way over and stood under her dangling feet. I raised me head and showed her me best smile.

"Good day to ye, young lady. I hope yer havin' a fine time makin' yer way across the island."

"I'm managing on my own, thank you very much. And you can put your hat back on because I know you're not a real gentleman. You're not even a gentle pirate!"

"Fair enough." It was easier just putting me hat back atop the crown of me head and trying to keep the smile. "Say, just wonderin' if ye've had the good fortune o' runnin' into Fernobarb or his handy li'l black jumpers. I'm sure thar happy to have a young visitor like yerself."

"No, I haven't seen him, and I don't care about him. I'm fast and small, so he can't find me, and even if he does . . . well, I'll find a way to take care of myself. So you can just go back to whatever it was you were doing."

"That's just the thing, Penny. I'm workin' on a new project and I think I might be askin' for yer help."

The li'l lady almost let a smile loose from her lips. I could tell she liked the idea that I was needing her. "Oh, really. You mean the meanest pirate of all time can't take care of himself?"

"I can, but, ye see, the problem is I need a hand with a task that might be just right fer ye. Are ye willin' to help?"

"And what is this task?"

"It's a difficult one, to be sure. And I present it to ye with the greatest o' hesitation, considerin' I've just met ye and I can't confirm whether or not yer capable of followin' through."

Penny stood tall on the branch. "Oh, I'm capable." She latched herself on to the trunk and spiraled her way up to a higher limb. "Redbeard, how are you ever going to know if you don't just spit it out and ask me?"

"All right then, I'll put it simple. I need ye, young Penny, to guard me beloved ship, the mighty *Picaroon.*"

"The whole ship?" Her eyes got big. I could see her try to pull back her excitement.

"That's right. Yer eyes watchin' over every last board."

"And why can't you handle it yourself?"

"Well, because . . . because I've got another job to do."

"And what's your job?"

"It's me own private job and I can't speak of it." I crossed me arms and leaned back so I could keep a sharp eye on her.

"Redbeard, how do you expect me to help if you won't even tell me what you're up to?"

"It's a matter o' me own safety and livelihood, li'l miss. Besides, we're wastin' plenty o' time talkin' about guardin' me ship while me ship sits thar all alone. I don't much see the sense in that. So why don't ye come down from thar and we can continue this li'l debate back at the ship."

"If we go back there now, you'll force me to help you against my will. That's what you do to all your crews." She snapped a small twig off the branch where she sat and threw it at me. I saw it coming and, with a quick side-step, was able to get out of the way.

"No, I won't."

"Yes, you will."

"Look here, I can't tell ye me task fer good reasons, and ye'll have to trust the fact, Penny. And since ye've decided to fend fer yerself without me help, I figure it's no business of yers what I do!"

"Fine, if you won't tell me, then I won't help."

Li'l Whisker, I wanted nothing more than to walk away from her right then and thar, but I reminded meself that finding a home and building a raft to carry Penny off the island were impossible without having someone to look over me treasure. "If ye must know, I can give ye a li'l hint, but that be it."

With that, she leapt from the tree to a flowered vine. After sliding halfway down, she watched the white petals shower round me. "All right, let's hear it, and I'll decide whether or not it's good enough for me to help."

"If that's what yer after, then I'll give ye the best hint I can muster." I knew I had her in the palm of me hand with what was about to spill from me lips. "Me task, Penny, is a surprise designed especially for yerself. How do ye like that?"

I didn't bother telling what kind of surprise it was, and

as long as she didn't ask, I wasn't under any obligation to rightly state whether it fell in the good or bad catergory. Even if she did ask, I could answer either way, for while she might be thinking the raft a bad surprise, I could safely and honestly slip it into the good category.

She stared down at me for a moment, then closed her eyes and shook her head. "No, I don't believe you, Redbeard. You're just saying that to trick me into helping you."

"But it's true! I'm workin' on a surprise fer ye. Let me put it this way. If, when I am done, ye do not have yer own personal surprise to keep fer yourself, then I will present ye with the greatest gift I could give."

"What's that?"

"The deed to the *Picaroon*."

"You don't have the deed, Redbeard. The ship was given to you because you scared the poor people of Crook Haven and they were afraid of you coming back—I know all about that."

"That Googler sure does have a mouth on him, don't he? Well, fine, then. I can't be presentin' ye with the deed, but ye have me word that the ship will be yers if I don't provide ye with a surprise."

"How do I know I can trust you?"

"Ye have me word, and that's all I can provide. If I go back on it, then ye'll never have to trust it again. That's how it works in the real world, missy. Ye learn who ye can trust and who ye can't."

She mulled it over while she swung her legs back and forth. I stepped away, giving her a moment of privacy. Soon I heard her sliding down the rest of the vine. She headed straight for me while wiping the dirt from her brown overalls. "Fine, Redbeard, you've got a deal. Let's go before I change my mind."

"Ladies first." I moved to the side and let her lead the way back to the *Picaroon*. And thar I positioned her directly in front of the stairs heading into the hallway 'fore me cabin. I gave her a bushel of spongefruit to keep her belly full while she stood lookout. And then I set about me task of gathering the tumble tree and securing its base to withstand the ocean's sometimes unmerciful tide. All the while, I knew I'd have to work quickly and keep a sharp eye out for ideal spots that I might be converting into me own personal Fundorado home.

Day 5

Building Penny's li'l raft took longer than I expected. Before I knew it, I felt the warmth of the setting sun against me back as I continued working. I had uprooted one of the tumble trees and lugged it to a hidden stretch of the beach, out of young Penny's field of vision. I was making several trips up to the edge of the jungle, where thar be a cluster of curious trees with fat, thick leaves draped along strong, bending branches. I broke 'em off in bunches, pressed the giant leaves against the base of the tumble tree and secured them with the wiry branches. I even gave an extra layer of protection up top just in case the li'l lady ran into rain. Every now and again I'd head over to the *Picaroon* to check on Penny and make sure she was sticking to her job. Every time, she'd hear me coming and yell out the same thing: "I'm still here, Redbeard. And yes, I'm still awake, so you can get back to my surprise."

The li'l pest impressed me with her stamina. I figured if she could last through the night, then I could too. So I kept working. And just as the first rays of sun started breaking over the horizon, I put the finishing touches on me work. That tumble tree was watertight and guarded against the rolling waves that would soon be lapping up against it. I pushed it to the water's edge, then bounded back to me ship to fetch Penny, the whole time wondering how I was going to explain the situation to her.

Li'l Whisker, it's funny how fate works out sometimes, for when I got back to me ship, I saw that li'l lady had finally caved to one of the greatest temptations of 'em all: a good, hard sleep. I took it as a sign. She looked so peaceful, stretched out along the stairs with her head propped up on the deck, that I couldn't rightly wake her. I figured it best to let her drift off in her slumber. That way she couldn't put up a fight and it'd make me task just a wee bit easier. So I gently raised her up into me arms and started back to the tumble tree raft. A few times she stirred with her li'l head pressed against me husky chest, but she was too far off in dreamland to wake up.

Back at the cove, I set her inside the tumble tree so smoothly thar was nary a squeak or creak from her own personal li'l raft. I left some ship biscuits at her side so she'd have something to keep her belly full.

It be true that waking her and trying to explain me reasons for doing what I did would've been a mighty task, but I'd be lying to ye, Li'l Whisker, if I said sending her off while she slept so sweetly was easy. It weren't. In fact, it was the hardest thing I'd done since having to tell Googler he was demoted to lieutenant. It took every last bit of strength in me muscles to shove the vessel across the last patch of sand and into the water. And it took every last ounce of me determination to not jump in after her and pull her back. Li'l Whisker, Penny was a brave one, to be sure. Anyone who could survive the storms I survived on the way to Fundorado deserves a tip o' the hat. But I just couldn't stand the thought of the li'l one getting hurt on me watch. I lowered me head and closed me eyes, spending a moment by meself, hoping for the best and trusting that some good soul would scoop her out of the water. Then I turned me back and started to me ship, for it would've been too painful to stand thar any longer, watching her fade into the night.

The Day I Lost Track

'Tis the honest truth, thar be not a sweeter spot to wander than here on Fundorado Island. Despite the numberless days that I've been here, I've still yet to see more than a third of the land. Me days have been stuffed to bursting with jungles, looking-glass rivers, glowing sand, scrumptious fruits and, till yesterday, no sight of the monster, Fernobarb. Li'l Whisker, ye might be wondering what it was like after Penny left, and I don't mind telling it to ye straight. Whatever li'l pinches of sadness I felt drifted away, bit by bit, with each passing day.

After breakfast, I usually spent a solid three hours getting me treasure a wee bit closer to the cave just below the crystal mountaintop. At night I'd been stashing it away in a temporary hiding spot, making it impossible for any no-good key thief, evil beast or the like to keep track of its whereabouts.

The task of lugging it all the way to me desired spot was a true chore from the very beginning. I wouldn't have been able to move it a single foot if the shipwreck hadn't busted a gaping hole in the wall of me chamber. I pushed against the chest, sliding it across the squeaking floor planks.

Up the beach I hauled me treasure day after day, creating a miniature road in the sand that snaked all the way down to the wrecked ship. What a load she was! Thank goodness I didn't take all the coins.

One morning I heaved the chest up and propped its enormous weight on me shoulders. Bending under the trunk, I stood at the mouth of the jungle. The veil of vines blocked me view of the cave, but I pressed onward, knowing I had found the perfect hideaway. While I was making me way through the thickest part of the trees, me boot got caught in the tangled web of roots and I stumbled to the ground, dropping the chest just in front of me. It seemed impossible that I'd be able to haul the treasure all the way up to that cave, but I had all the time in the world.

After I got the hang of handling the heavy load, I was able to cover ground more quickly. A few days later I came upon a bridge that arched over the strangest river I'd ever seen. Do you know what I saw below the surface, Li'l Whisker? I saw me face. And just above that, the treasure. And just above that, the gathering clouds in the sky. It wasn't just a reflection glistening in yer average river. It was a giant looking glass that had melted into the riverbed, filling it with the steady current of a silvery flow. That's right, the water was a mirror.

It seemed like an ideal place to stop and rest. After so many trips with that heavy chest, me back needed a good stretch every now and again. Besides, I couldn't help kneeling down and scooping me hand into the water. Even the shallow pool in me palm formed a liquid looking glass.

The bright water rushed under me, carrying a twisted

branch blooming with that tasty cinnamon fruit. As the current lured the fruits off to the left, a peculiar sight commanded me attention: on the other side of the river, a different branch was coming against the current. Were me eyes to be believed? Was the mighty river actually flowing two ways at once? Well, indeed she was. But this bit of water had even more tricks up her sleeve, for in the middle where the two currents met, bubbling whirlpools sputtered and popped, arguing over what water went in which direction, churning in front of me like hurricanes all lined up in a row. It was a sight to see, Li'l Whisker, and it became one of me favorite spots to sit at noontime with me feet cooling off in the water, taking notes on me adventures.

And some of me exploring led me face to face with the ugly mug o' danger. The most spine-curling moment of 'em all came one afternoon when I was wandering about the wilderness maybe three miles south of the *Picaroon*'s new dock. A snake of rapidly changing colors slithered across me foot. At once, I noticed a curious variety of tree. It bent this way and that like a crooked wire. On the upper bunch of its twisted branches hung hundreds of long sprouts. From behind the trunk, Marmoona stepped, his hooked staff raised high. He dragged the crook along a branch and caught the pods as they fell to the ground. The lengthy-tailed Whip Cat licked its paws far above the tallest reaches of the tree. Across a field, I spotted a few felines just like the Whip Cat. They lounged in a nice patch of shade, mewling, and grooming each other. The Whip Cat spotted them too. He jumped down from one branch to the next but froze as Marmoona stared into his eyes and pounded his staff in the dirt. When the cat settled in a narrow fork of the tree, the speckle-belly went back to work on the sprouts.

I kept exploring. At a point, trees stopped growing. The ground was hard, black and bubbled over. Me nose twinged at the charred scent circling round. Ripped in a random line, the lumpy black land ceased entirely. Beyond the crumbling edge, a flaming orange gush burped and groaned. An enormous lake o' lava stretched in front of me. Its spinning fumes were swaying over the fiery surface. From the looks of it, I could cut me way across the lake on some black stepping-stones afloat in a row all the way across the liquid flame. But, Lil' Whisker, that was a risk for a braver fool than I.

A heart-stopping howl echoed over the lava, hanging low and slow like a spilling fog. I became still and scanned me surroundings for the source. I squatted low to the ground, for thar was nothing near to hide behind. Beyond the lake's murky smoke mask, I saw it, coming from the north. Again it unleashed its howl, a rumble that escaped the heat o' the hereafter yet somehow ended up in the pit o' me belly. Three slender critters zipped along the lava. They bounced up, skipping as they ran. Thar long bodies shined like sleek fur coats tightly wound around boomerangs. A jumble of stone stretched across the animals' path, and all three of them raced to it, hiding in its dark hollows.

Between the sinking sun and meself, Fernobarb came into view. Li'l Whisker, the monster that plodded forth would give even the bogeyman himself a reason to sleep with the lamp lit. Across the smoky black sand the silhouette patrolled. An escape dinghy stuffed with one man too many wouldn't be much larger than this shadowy beast.

Slowly it stretched toward the opposite end of the lake. As it tramped onward, the strange outline of its body took shape. A thatch of bristles drooped from the bottom of an ample chin. Trailing behind the bruising form, a thick, thorned tail hovered just above the ridges in the glint. Rising in the air, a clump of pointed lumps crowned its massive head. From a hole in that bony mass, a single feather o' flame flickered right out of its skull. Fernobarb was hammered out of pure muscle and yet slinked through the pit like an alley cat 'tween the barrels and boxes of a blackened back street.

From the rocks one of the three furry things made a run for it. The others stayed hidden deep in the stone crevasse. Me eyes crossed at the speed of Fernobarb's reaction. In a blur, its matted front paws extended to pull the ground under it—a single stride seemed to be almost double its entire length. Thar weren't no two ways about it . . . this evil beast was the fastest being I'd ever seen. It could outrun anything.

Thar was nothing fair in the chase. Fernobarb was on the trio even before I knew he was after them. One powerful claw pierced one of the critter's tails. The odd thing was, Fernobarb didn't stop the slowest animal—it stopped the fastest! Dull cries and whimpers escaped from the poor fella as he rolled along the ground, his tail tethered under Fernobarb's claw. Far in the rock, the other two ran from the scene. Just under the beast's wet nose, the little critter gulped for air. With a shrinking glare the beast stared its meal down. An anxious grumble shook the graying skies. The evil thing roared long 'n' loud 'n' shot a sticky gray tongue over the li'l guy. As quickly as it came out, it was sucked back in, while the small critter jerked in a fit. The jaws clamped down. The beast tossed its head back and swallowed its victim whole.

At the outcropping of rocks, the vile monster peered down the crevasse. It belted out a juicy snort, then took three very deep and long breaths before spinning a miniature tornado from its fat nose. The tiny storm twirled over the crevasse, pulling the other two critters from thar hiding spot. In two quick darts of the beast's tongue, the critters were gone.

Again Fernobarb began to prowl, crawling low against the earth. It snuck up onto the land's edge, pausing to draw in the scent of the air, its gaze simmering all the while on me side of the fire. Its muscles twitched in unison, and with one terrific leap, it was sailing over the lake. It skidded along the rocky shore. In a panic I hopped onto a stepping-stone before it had a chance to see me. first one stone, then a few more. The lake's scorching vapors enveloped me. I took off me hat and coat as sweat swam down me face.

I could hardly see the evil creature through the murk, but Fernobarb found some more prey. A large, fuzzy, striped creature (I've come to dub them Mackrains) ran as the savage monster ripped bites right out of him. Me left foot was covered in blisters while I crouched against the hot, floating stone. Fernobarb nudged the animal toward the lake with its gnashing bone snout. The striped creature tripped on its two front legs. In a blitz, Fernobarb charged at the animal. With its flame-topped head low to the ground, the vile devil rammed the poor critter to the center of the flaming lake. A shrieking whimper was extinguished in a blur of smoke.

How horrible for that innocent animal—but it was horrible for me, too, Lil' Whisker. The beast was so big, fiery ripples circled out from where it landed. The rings came by me, pulling the stepping-stones far apart. I was stranded in the midst of the glowing lake.

With Fernobarb long gone, I sat till nearly nightfall. Me mind was fuzzy from the lack of water. In the sky, a giant silvery bird flew. I swung me coat in the air, hollering up to her. In a single motion, she unleashed her mammoth wings, dove down and skimmed through the cloudy curtain. Still I clung to the stone tightly as a clam. In the lake's burning reflection I caught a flash of feathers, and in an instant I was out of the pickle. Held in the giant feet of an even gianter bird, I hung over the lava—me entire body still locked like a trap from shock.

We rose into the clouds. The low hum of the cottony feathers purred about me with each downward flap of those great wings. When hovering aloft like that, it's a tough chore not to imagine yerself as the sun smoldering over the land. The island stretched out under us: Fundorado, in all its wondrous majesty. The teal waters o' the sea hugged the glittery beaches and jagged rock coasts. Curling capes jutted out. I was parched. I was hungry. I was tired. And that's all I can remember.

Come dawn I awoke in a nest of branches, and Li'l Whisker, it really was a nest I was sleeping in—a great nest like a giant bed. And the story gets even better, for on the twiggy edge a whole mess o' bright, mouth-watering fruits and berries were laid out just for me. Thar I was, curled up in the cozy bed as the tremendous gray bird nudged the fruit toward me with her glossy hooked beak. At the tips of her wings I could see the soft pink that had once soaked every last feather, but now she was an older, gentle bird, and the silvery layer had spread across most of her coat.

Her eyes stuck on me till I finished every last bit, and when I was done, she gently lifted me in her feet and carried me over Fundorado Island, back to the crystal sands where I left the *Picaroon.* All the while, she let out a soothing tune of "Gaya . . . Gaya . . ." So I reckoned I'd call her Gaya Bird.

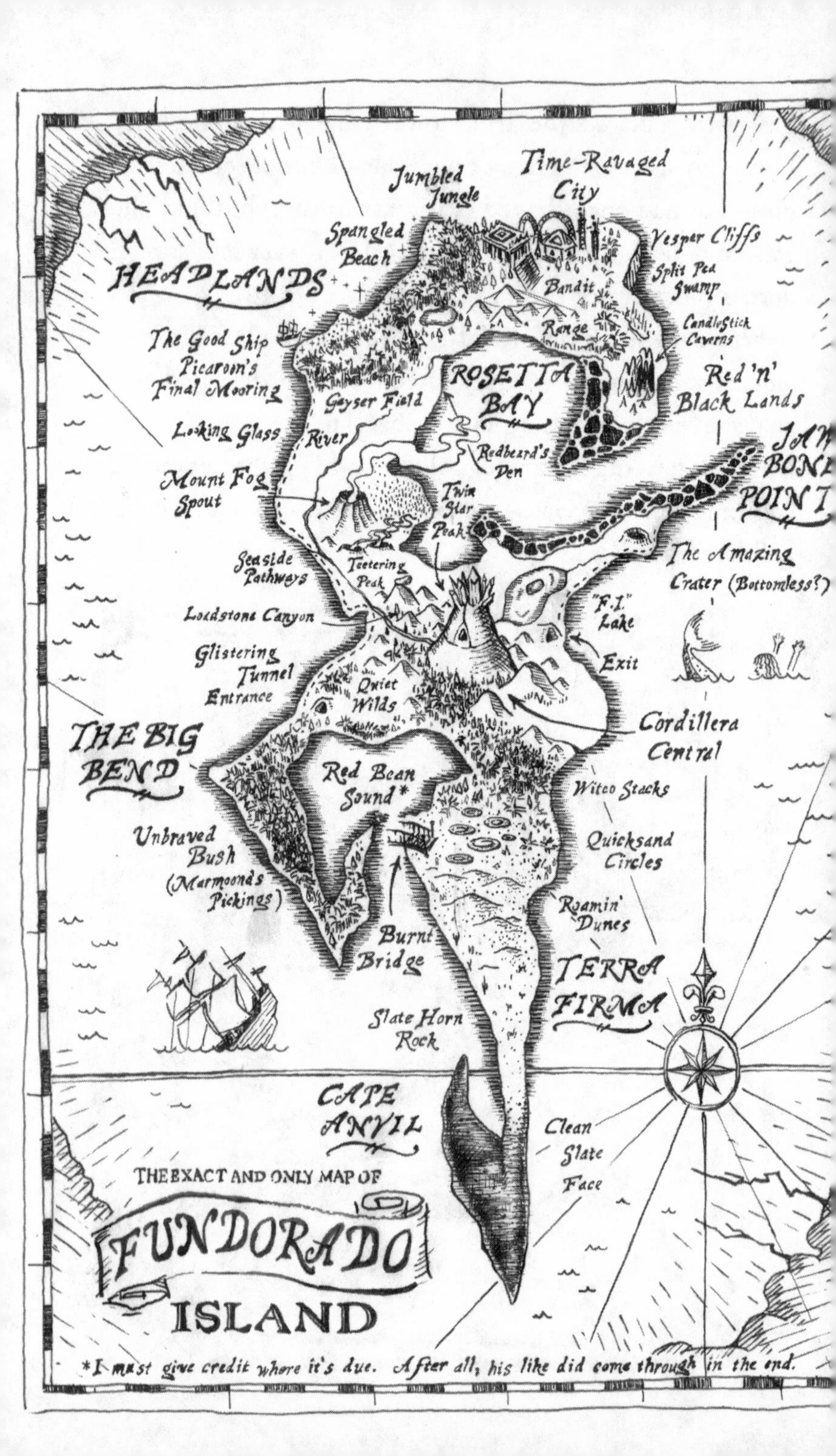
Time-Ravaged City
Jumbled Jungle
Spangled Beach
Vesper Cliffs
Split Pea Swamp
HEADLANDS
Bandit Range
Candlestick Caverns
The Good Ship Picaroon's Final Mooring
ROSETTA BAY
Red 'n' Black Lands
Geyser Field
Looking Glass River
Redbeard's Den
Mount Fog Spout
Twin Star Peak
Seaside Pathways
Teetering Peak
The Amazing Crater (Bottomless?)
Loadstone Canyon
"F.I." Lake
Glistering Tunnel Entrance
Quiet Wilds
Exit
THE BIG BEND
Cordillera Central
Red Bean Sound*
Witco Stacks
Unbraved Bush (Marmoond's Pickings)
Quicksand Circles
Roamin' Dunes
Burnt Bridge
TERRA FIRMA
Slate Horn Rock
CAPE ANVIL
Clean Slate Face
THE EXACT AND ONLY MAP OF
FUNDORADO
ISLAND
*I must give credit where it's due. After all, his like did come through in the end.

The trip back to the grounded ship was incredible. High above the treetops and glistening shores we sailed, gliding inside the curves of the breeze. Far below, I saw much of the island that I had already covered. The glowing red lake behind us, the Jumbled Jungle, winding rivers and the squared-faced creatures' web of odd ropes stretched across the cluster of hills. In the middle of it all, a string of mountains extended to the north end of the island. The jewel of the range was Twin Star Peak, with its crystal top towering over all the other peaks.

I was set on the *Picaroon*'s deck and waved to Gaya Bird as I watched her disappear over the pointed cliffs.

Li'l Whisker, I spent the better part of the next morning trying to retrace me days so I could be more precise in telling ye how things were going and how long they were taking. But the fact is, it wasn't possible to keep track of time on Fundorado, and I finally came to terms with that. Marking the days and hours just didn't make much sense when thar was so much to do and so much to explore. So you'll have to keep hold of me coattails and follow along. Thar was no way of logging every inch. I decided I'd best enjoy the land and keep moving forward.

And I was doing just that. Making good progress on me new home, which, I'd like to tell ye, I called Redbeard's Den. I found quite the spot, Li'l Whisker. Me abode was to be carved out of the roots of a giant tree at the back end of the Symphony Selva, the family of timber that makes a delightful tune when the wind cuts through the holes that pepper the trunks. If ye fancy, ye can even add to the music by takin' a stick to the branches and strikin' the jangly clusters of hollowed-out berries. That way ye get a full orchestra.

Me treasure, too, was inching li'l by li'l closer to that glorious tip of Twin Star Peak that rose high into the sky, giving me a way to keep track of me steps.

All was going smoothly until I was over near the hop rocks, gathering some medium-sized sticks to patch up a hole near the entrance to me den. I heard a voice coming from farther up the bank of the river. Right away I recognized that uneven timber and knew it was Marmoona. I hunkered down and waited for him to make his way through the trees, out into the open where I could see him. Suddenly I heard a second voice, softer and harder to make out. I gripped the sides of the giant boulder that I was hiding behind, a li'l touch of uneasiness swelling in me as I waited to see just who the speckle-belly was talking to. Li'l Whisker, I'm sure it'll fill you with as much shock as it did me to find out that the second voice belonged to none other than young Penny! Me eyes grew so big at the sight of her, it felt like they might just bust out of thar sockets and tumble into the water. She had woken up on the tumble tree raft! And survived! And come back to Fundorado!

I threw meself to the ground and looked for the nearest cover, which happened to be a hollowed-out log. Let me tell ye, Li'l Whisker, I am not a slim man, but I did somehow manage to wedge me body all the way in thar, clear out of sight. And it was a good thing too, for Marmoona and Penny walked straight in me direction and took a seat on the log—right on top of me!

Turns out I wasn't alone in the hollow tree. I noticed a stinging stench wafting from the far end. I was sharing me hiding spot with a pudgy pink ball o' critter. (I've seen a few more since then. Thar pink skin gets boiled under the sun, so they like to keep hidden in the shade. If they weren't so smelly, I might get friendlier with them shade-grazers.)

The speckle-belly and the stowaway sounded like they were enjoying each other's company. I tried to spy details here and thar through small splits in the thick wood. Oh, how it stank! I shoved two fingers in me nostrils to cork the pink stinker's reek out of me nose. Penny even had a pitcher of water in her hands, and it seemed as if she was helping Marmoona with some of his solitary island chores I've seen him doing so many times. I could barely make out what they were saying over the sound of the water flowing by.

"Where does this water come from, Marmoona?" The li'l lady looked up at the critter, clinging to his side as she awaited his response.

"From the lost, lost city. No humans there now. Not today, not tomorrow. It will be safest if humans stay away from there for good."

"Because of that Fernobarb?"

"Sweet water's for the island. Not for the humans like that one. You go to take a drink from the well and he comes to find you before the drink hits your belly."

"But it's so good, Marmoona! Will you bring me some every day? Just a little. Fernobarb will never know about it, and I won't tell Redbeard. If he knows, then he'll want some too, and he'll probably drink it all up in a couple of days."

It wasn't easy, Li'l Whisker, sitting thar, listening to feisty Penny's opinions. Especially considering how all I wanted to do was jump to me feet and ask her what the fickle finger of fate had done to get her back on the island. But even if I had shouted to her, she probably wouldn't have heard it, for the two of 'em got up and started farther down the bank of the river. I followed 'em, staying a ways back so they wouldn't hear me. Me steps have been on the noisy side, Li'l Whisker. It ain't easy making me way around Fundorado terrain gracefully with one of me poor feet having to make every step without a boot thar to protect it.

Soon enough, Penny and Marmoona parted ways. But before they did, they shared a good laugh, and the li'l lady threw her arms around the yellow belly, giving the critter a mighty hug. I didn't like it much, the sight o' the two o' them being so friendly without me knowing about it. I needed some answers, and I wasn't willing to wait.

I had to track one of them, and I decided to keep pace with Penny. Me first and foremost question was how in blazes she had gotten back on the island, and it's always best to get the answer straight from the source.

Me task proved to be a li'l trickier than I was expecting on account of the fact that young Penny had obviously spent some time learning the ins and outs of some of the island and the fact that she liked moving quickly and nimbly. She dashed along with Marmoona's Whip Cat scrambling behind her the whole way. I was doing just fine keeping up until she crossed over to a part of the island I hadn't yet seen. Over beyond the miniature horses thar were a cluster of oversized bushes, full and wavy. They were fat down at the base, and narrowed to a point the higher they climbed. They varied in size, but most came up past me chest. Before I knew it I was zigzagging 'tween 'em, trying to find Penny, as she had wandered out of sight. I was moments away from giving up when I heard her li'l voice.

"Blackbeard . . . oh, Blackbeard!"

"Very funny, young Penny. But ye know very well that ain't me name."

"I know that. I just thought I'd get a rise out of you."

"And so ye did. Now would ye mind revealin' yer present location?"

"What, you mean you can't see me?"

"'Fraid not."

"Well, why don't you look a little closer?"

I hunched down and moved as swiftly as I could 'tween the meandering trails that separated the bushes. Still she was nowhere to be seen. "I'm lookin', but ye seem to be hidin' away somewhere."

"It's fun, isn't it, Captain? You have to find me."

"Fine, missy. If ye ain't goin' to tell me where ye are, will ye mind answerin' another question fer me?"

"Maybe. Depends on the question. Are you wondering whether or not I liked my surprise?"

"Yer surprise?" I ran me fingers through me beard, trying to follow her train of thought.

"Yes, the raft you built for me."

"Ah, of course! Yer li'l raft. Yes, I do believe that was going to be me question. So tell me, Penny, what'd ye think?"

"Well, I did like it. That doesn't mean you weren't mean to your crew. And it doesn't mean you haven't been a little bit grumpy with me. But I did like the ride. Oh, I did very much!"

"Glad to hear it." I cleared me throat and tried to form me questions carefully. "And just where did yer ride take ye, if ye don't mind me askin'? I'm just wantin' to make sure it worked out as I planned."

"Around the entire island, silly. Oh, Redbeard, there is so much you have to see!"

"And ye weren't worried about driftin' too far out, were ye? Maybe even losin' sight of Fundorado altogether?"

She let out a li'l laugh from her hiding spot. "That's impossible. Haven't you learned anything here yet, Redbeard?"

"I hardly think it's impossible, miss. When I set ye in the water, I was expectin'. . . ah, I knew it might be a possibility. That's all I'm sayin'. It was a worry in the back of me mind and I'm glad to see ye stuck close by."

"That's sparkletricity, Redbeard. You should know that by now. Maybe if you were a little nicer to Marmoona, he'd let you know all about it."

"Don't ye worry, Penny, I know what this here island's sparkletricity is. Rosetta spoke of it long before you were gallivantin' around with the speckle-belly. It's exactly what landed me here, and it's exactly what I've been soakin' up since me first day on Fundorado. Whenever yer in a pinch or in need of something, it's thar to take care of ye."

I heard a thud in the dirt just behind me.

"Like that?"

I looked back, and do you know what I saw? It was me missing boot! Lying right thar in front of me naked foot. As I reached down to grab it, I heard a soft li'l whisper coming from the bush just in front of me. When I gave it a closer look, I saw Penny's bright eyes peering at me from behind the green shoots.

"Me boot? How'd ye get me boot?"

"I just climbed up in the tree and brought it down."

"Ye climbed all the way up thar by yer lonesome?"

"I don't need any help climbing. I can climb anything faster than anyone!"

"Ye climbed all the way up thar for me?"

"I figured one good surprise deserves another."

"Indeed, missy. That's awful friendly of ye to look at it that way."

"Well, it's true."

"Is this yer way of sayin' ye'd like to be me friend? I ain't quite sure, seein' how I've never done this before."

"Okay, Redbeard. I'm in if you're in. Friends." Then her hand poked out and her li'l finger extended to beckon me toward her. I pushed past green shoots and made me way into the hollowed-out interior of the bush. I had to hunker down so me head didn't hit the top of the teepee. She sat in the middle with a smile plastered across her face and asked me to join her. I could tell she had been staying thar awhile, for it was set up cozy-like, with big leaf pillows, a wooden bowl of spongefruit and a bouquet of wildflowers she had gathered. Thar was even a wooden knife she had fashioned by herself.

"How'd ye find this place, Penny?"

"You just have to go looking. Marmoona helped me find it. He told me it's related to the tree you used to make my raft. You can't search anywhere on this island without stumbling upon some kind of surprise, Redbeard."

"Truest words ye ever did speak, young Penny. . . . Penny, what be yer whole name?"

"You know my first name."

"Right, indeed I do."

"So why do you need to know my surname?"

"Well, for when I be wanting to call to ye official-like."

"That's boring, using my real name. You of all people, Redbeard, should know that." She had me thar, Li'l Whisker. I sat trying to stutter out a response, but she continued before I could form one. "Do you know what, Redbeard? I think you might be right. Maybe it wouldn't hurt if I told you my name. Or even better, I could make up a fake one, like Gertrude von Buttersnip, just to keep you guessing."

Of course she was trying to hide her grin, but her teeth kept sneaking out. Her smile then turned into laughter, spilling out in fits and starts. Between the jolly outbursts she quizzed, "So . . . do you want to call me . . . Miss von Buttersnip?"

At this she erupted into a flurry of silliness, nearly rocking her entire body onto the mud shoots where she slept.

"Now, now, Miss von Buttersnip, if given the opportunity to make a choice, I would surely settle on the real McCoy."

Her giggles petered out and she wiped the tickled tears from her eyes. She stood up tall, her head raised to the sky so she could peer at me all the way down her narrow nose. She drenched her voice in authority. "Are you sure, then, Captain Redbeard, that this is your decision?"

"As certain as can be, miss."

Still she pumped the pomp in her voice. "Then let it be stated to both the left and right ear of Captain Redbeard that from this day forward he is permitted to call me by my true, full name . . . Penny Morun."

She waved her hands to and fro, humming to some dreamed-up orchestra.

"So that's the name yer poor mother and father are cryin' over at this very instant, is it?"

The smile disappeared from young Miss Morun's face, and her body seemed to sink another inch into the floor of the hut-bush. "Don't worry, Redbeard, I don't think of home too much. I don't miss it because it doesn't miss me . . . except for my dad, I'm sure he misses me. When I had to live with the banker and his wife, I asked about my father, and they said he was visiting the pearly gates. The groundskeeper of Sand Dollar Square Park told me that my dad was called to the great blue. Pearls and blue. It sounds like the ocean, doesn't it?"

"Aye, a wee bit—"

"I know he won't come back, but still, I want to get as close to where he is as possible. It was more than adventure that I was looking for when I snuck aboard the *Picaroon*."

"Ah, ye've run away, Penny? A lass with no home to call her own? Me apologies to ye about yer father. It's an ache ye can bet yer eyeteeth dear Redbeard understands."

Penny reached behind her for a couple o' wooden cups and a small gourd pitcher and poured each of us a bit of pulpy sugar bee juice.

"Ye have it hard, Penny. At least we pirates be lucky when it comes to home, for our home be whatever's in our chests. Why, we could take our homes around the world if we like, ain't that the life?"

"And I suppose you could sail the seven seas without once getting homesick."

"Or seasick!"

As we shared a hearty laugh, I felt something making its way across me back. When I started to turn to see what was thar, Penny hollered me way, "Black jumpers! Stay right where you are, Redbeard. Don't move!" She inched toward a small cup hidden behind the bowl of spongefruit. After slowly reaching into the cup with her hand, she quickly brought out her wetted fingers, flicking 'em at the jumper on me shoulder. When the moisture hit the thing, it immediately fell from me coat and hit the ground.

"It's dead!"

"Yep."

"How'd ye kill it?"

"With my spitflower poison."

"Where'd ye get it?"

"I made it."

"Well, what's in it?"

"It's got the nectar from a spitflower and another secret ingredient."

"What be yer secret ingredient?"

"It wouldn't be secret if I told you."

"I see ye can be trusted with a secret. I like that." I reached me arms behind me, trying to relax with a full breath, knowing I had just escaped a wee bit of danger. When me hand slid across the base of the hut-bush, it hit up against something fat and furry in the darkened corner. A loud shriek filled the space and I jumped forward. Penny laughed and gave me a good smack across me husky back. "You silly goose, it's only the Whip Cat."

At her words, the li'l critter crawled out and snuggled up against the li'l lady.

"I see ye've made friendly with him."

"Marmoona lets me look after him every now and then. I told him about how I still can't find Juliet, and he said he didn't want me feeling too lonely."

Li'l Whisker, Googler's rat had completely left me mind. Seeing the sadness swell up in young Penny's eyes, I knew I'd have to fess up. Thar be some moments in life when it comes clear that ye can't dance around the truth any longer. "Look here, Penny. Some things be easier to say than others. This here just might be the hardest of 'em all, but I can't avoid it for another minute. I need to let you know that Juliet is dead."

"What? How do you know that?"

"I was thar when it happened."

"Where is she?"

"That be what I'm tellin' ye, she ain't with us anymore. I was tryin' to look after her for ye. After readin' the note, I knew ye'd been entrusted with her safekeepin', so I figured I'd track her down and make sure she stayed close by. But, Penny, I'm sorry to say, lookin' after animals has never come easy to me. I didn't know rightly how to care for her, and I'm 'fraid she passed on under me watch. I haven't been able to find the words for ye till now, because I knew no matter how I arranged the facts, they'd break yer heart."

At that, the Whip Cat jumped in Penny's lap and rubbed its nose to her chin, almost like it knew what we were saying. The young girl lay down with her furry friend pressed up against her belly. I sat thar watching the two of 'em fade off to sleep together. I didn't know what to do, but I couldn't leave her by her lonesome in that sad state and thar wasn't much else I could say. So I took off me boots and settled in for the night. I learned a valuable lesson thar with me new friend in her hut-bush. When Fundorado puts its sparkletricity to work, thar be no arguing with it. The island had decided it wanted Penny to stay, and I wasn't about to say otherwise.

Turns out mud tubes don't make a half-bad bed. In the morning I stretched me arms in an earnest yawn and hopped to me feet. From the slits in Penny's hut-bush door, I saw the meadow already beaming under the early Fundorado sun. "Lucky Penny," I chirped, just loudly enough for her sleeping ear to hear. "Lucky Penny, wake up."

She pulled her grass-stuffed leaf pillow over her head. A moment later a muffled voice emerged. "Do you remember how I saved you from the black jumpers?"

"Don't ye mean how ye saved the black jumpers from me? Why, I would've turned them inside out if ye hadn't stepped in with that spitflower poison."

She threw her leaf pillow at me, spilling grass

everywhere. "You're a stinker, Redbeard." As she gave the Whip Cat a scratch on his back, she plainly offered, "Redbeard, I'll forgive you for what you did to my little Juliet. But I want you to know that I'll never let you keep an eye on this furry boy." She smushed his face 'tween her hands and blew li'l kisses at his long whiskers.

"Right ye are, missy. We've got ourselves an agreement."

I raked a finger in me mouth to remove a bitter blade of grass. "Hey, what do ye say to a cool sip o' that sweet water ole Marmoona's been hidin'?"

"At the ruins? Are you mad? Marmoona said it's dangerous. He said, 'Trouble is there.' "

I sat on the end of the mud-tube bed. "Be ye the same li'l stove-away who made it through a treacherous storm at sea?"

"Of course."

"And be ye also the girl who survived the tree-crashin' shipwreck?"

"Yes, yes, yes. That's me! Penny!"

Me cheeks made great room for a smile. "Ye mean *Lucky* Penny. Yer right, that was ye, but who was it who was with ye the whole time?"

"Marmoona!" she squealed in hysterics.

"Sharp as daggers, ye are." I lobbed the now half-filled pillow her way. "No, ye silly munchkin. It was me—I was with ye the whole time. And I'll be with ye at the ruins, just the same."

"What if Marmoona gets angry?"

"If Marmoona is angry, then I'll be angry too—angry that ye told him we went. I can't figure any other way he'd find out."

Penny flung one o' the *Picaroon*'s blankets aside and said with an impish grin, "I won't tell him."

Our trail threaded through giant pointed trees. Nestled in one was a fat yellow bird. It sat, beak agape, with its three li'l chicks tweedling aloud thar yellow-feathered melodies. We stepped a wee bit closer and the mouth snapped shut in silence. We backed off a pace or two; then the beak opened and the singing resumed. Penny had a hoot listening and repeated the process no fewer than seven times. No doubt exhausted, the bird sealed its mouth and flew to a more private part o' the tree. We continued on our way to the ruins. Penny whistled the yellow birds' catchy tune, and I kept the tempo with me hands clapping.

What a hike we footed! For a trip made for the sole purpose of getting sweet water, we sure stopped a lot to drink from the murky creeks and falls that lined our path. Penny was thirsty as a sailor, bless her heart. I, on the other hand, was saving me thirst for the good stuff.

Penny grabbed me arm. "Can you see it? I think I see it!"

Before I could breathe an answer, the li'l stove-away dashed through the brush and down the rocky bluff. I could see it now: an ancient city. Its staggering beauty humbled me to me boots—both of 'em.

All along the flat north end of the island the stone city stretched. A great wall o' stones and corkscrew palisades stood guard. Nary a living soul walked the streets. Every step, every doorway and every window was empty. Penny stalled, frozen in the dirt road that led to the ruins. She quietly asked, "Do you think we should?"

"Aye, we should," I hollered back to her. "I think we should race!"

She quickly kicked up a cloud of dust as she rushed past me to the pillars of a massive gate. One side was shut. The other, tipping from a single hinge, lay planted wide open in the ground. We entered the city cautiously but soon found ourselves popping into this doorway and that, fully enchanted by the powdery stone remnants of this once mighty place. Burgundy ivy hung from everything. Even deep inside the buildings, the vines dropped from forgotten cracks to strangle the handsome furniture.

"My word, this one is different. . . . How stunning!" The girl spoke in awe.

I stepped out from a century's overgrowth in the courtyard to see what had nabbed her attention. Tall columns surrounded the spice-scented garden. They were made o' dark webbed iron, separated by bright chunks o' color—lavender, sky and violet. The columns were hollow, creating a striking effect as the sun shone. It looked as if the tall supports were lit from within. Penny wanted to explore its winding staircase interior, but I was so parched from the trek, I needed to wet me whistle first. "We'll get what we came for, then we'll play."

At the far end of the dusty road a few buckets were placed around a short stump of stone. Penny pointed. "See the buckets? That must be the well!"

We ran to the stump and I lowered one down a hole in the center. Using me shoulder for support, she propped herself on the edge and gazed into the darkness.

"Look how far down it goes, Penny." I hoisted the overflowing bucket back out and we took turns sipping from it.

"It tastes like a diamond," Penny said, wiping her mouth with her arm.

"What a perfect fit for the flavor. Diamond water it is."

"This one doesn't know what to feel!" Marmoona was standing right behind us!

Penny dropped the bucket and I kicked it behind the well. The li'l lady whispered up to me, "Here's the trouble."

"This one can't have you here! Important to go. Go fast! Come with this one."

The speckle-belly took us down the dirt road, back to the ivy-covered city. "These buildings are no more lived in. Those ones were just like you." He gestured with his painted staff in our direction. "So long ago, so very long ago, those ones were here alive in the city. So loud those ones were. The mean one, Fernobarb, didn't want to share Fundorado with them."

We climbed the broad steps of a grandly fluted palace. "This one to show you. Come this way." The speckle-belly took us to a great room lined with human statues. Men and women danced on thar toes, gracefully still in the silence.

Penny tugged on the mane of hair running down Marmoona's back. "What's that funny writing on the wall?"

Flowing in beautiful wedges, the letters wound round the tops of the tall columns. "That is the secret language of the gone people. Sad news, those ones had. Fernobarb hated them in so many awful ways. That one will hate you, too, right here and now."

"But, Marmoona, we didn't do anything to be hated." Young Penny couldn't see the sense in it all, and I couldn't blame her.

"Fernobarb makes the storms when humans are here. That one wants the island all to itself."

With that, an uncomfortable wind laced round our faces. *Ssssshwuh,* it beat against our clothes.

"Oh, no! That one comes right after the weather it spoils. This one doesn't want you to be one of the gone people. You will be quiet now."

Our bellies rumbled from the roar. Fernobarb stormed down from the bluff.

"Quick, quick, bad ones—to the well!"

The evil beast charged closer still.

"No, in here! No time for you now!" Marmoona pushed us down the steps of the building. From our shelter we saw the poor speckle-belly try to fend off the beast. Fernobarb stepped on his staff, then chomped down on his leg, tearing it off just below the knee. Penny started to sob, and I didn't blame her one bit. The nasty creature tossed Marmoona aside and began ravaging our building. Columns snapped and walls buckled, spraying curtains of debris into the air. Lightning cracked.

"Penny, to the well!" I ordered. "Be brave, li'l one. Ye know how lucky ye are. I'll catch up to ye soon." She gave me a hug and bolted for the well.

Hiding in the wreckage, I waited for me chance. Fernobarb thrust a heavy-taloned paw into the ruins to get at me, but luckily, I was too far back. It paced to and fro, ready to cave the roof in over me head. It let out a wet howl, the same wet howl I remembered it releasing before blowing the tornado at the lava lake. This was it! As the horrible thing took its three long breaths, I sprinted out the side to the road and slung Marmoona over me back. I took two steps, stopped, leaned back and grabbed a piece of his staff. I turned me head to the speckle-belly. "Looks like we're off to the well."

A great clash rang out in the sky, and sheets of hot rain crashed in muddy pools along the dirt road. Fernobarb howled in rage right at the dripping brim o' me hat. As the speckle-belly bounced on me shoulder, a sparking bolt dove into a dirty puddle. I don't mind telling ye, I ran like a frightened cabin boy.

Diamond water doesn't come from just any old well, Li'l Whisker. At the bottom of the long chute, the well opened up to a cavernous chamber. Dripstones of blue and purple drooped from the ceiling. The drops fell—*ploink!*—and rippled away. With Marmoona on me back, I wrapped me legs around the rope 'n' slid down. Penny, already at the bottom, sat curled in the bow of a li'l rowboat. She was soaked to the core.

"Over here, Penny!" I whispered as loudly as I could. "Row the boat under the rope."

Lightning flashed outside. Marmoona gasped. Fernobarb jabbed a bony head down the well. Speckle-belly wailed, "This one sorry!"

Fernobarb's terrible mouth opened. It reared back and jumped at us. A strand o' tooth juice twirled from those trembling lips and landed across me nose.

"No, Penny. Use both oars!"

The frightened face disappeared from the opening. "I got it now. Hang in there, Marmoona." Penny powered toward the rope.

An amazing gust rushed down the well. Fernobarb's hungry teeth clamped down just inches from me fist. The rope was severed in his mouth. I hung with Marmoona just below Fernobarb's jaws. The beast threw its mouth into a wicked howl, our rope lodged in its gums 'tween two cold fangs. It stretched down farther into the well. But thanks to the rope, no matter how far the vile creature leaned, we were always just out of reach. Its flaming hot tongue darted at me hand. I slipped a bit and the rope shot loose. Marmoona landed in the rowboat. I didn't. Fernobarb, too big to fit in the well on account of those broad horns upon his head, wreaked havoc at the entrance. At least for the time being, we were safe from the rampage. I climbed into the boat and took over rowing duty.

I moved us along. Penny slept next to Marmoona, who, even in his sleep, winced from the pain in his leg. The cavern wound around with dizzying possibilities. But I didn't stop till I felt Penny 'n' the speckle-belly were safe, which happened to be at an underground iceberg. After mooring the boat, I unloaded the passengers. "This place looks safe," I said.

Penny scrunched her face. "This place looks cold."

Marmoona faded in 'n' out of wakefulness. "This one knows . . ." His breath was visible against the chill. "These ones are safe here. The bad one can't come here."

From an inside pocket, I pulled a flask and tipped it to

Marmoona's wide lips. "Me friend, have a li'l sip o' this." He drank it dry and plunged back to sleep.

A shivering Penny quizzed me. "What was in that thing?"

"Just some chocolate milk." I smiled and bundled me coat round her goose-bumped arms. "Do you want to help Marmoona?"

"How can I?" she wondered.

"Cut a strip o' cloth from the tail o' me coat. We're goin' to fix the speckle-belly's leg."

I removed all the splintered tips from the broken end of his staff. When Penny was finished with the piece o' cloth, I used her knife to cut a wedge from the staff. She proved to be a smart one, having thought to grab the blade when we left the hut bush.

"Ye see how the wood be higher on the two sides? Those parts are goin' to fit round his bone. Then we'll tie it tight. Tight like a . . . like a . . ." Me mind was obviously on too many things.

Lucky Penny was thar for me, though. "Maybe . . . like a clam?" Her hands out to her sides in question.

"We'll tie it tight like a clam."

We finished the job together. Afterward, the li'l girl fell right to sleep. Marmoona's pain finally began to fade. And I tried to fill me husky lungs with deep breaths. All the while, I wondered what our next step would be.

Over three days we hid in the frigid underground cavern. Young Penny was good enough to share the sweet, tangy berries she had stuffed away in her pockets. Thar was plenty o' time for sitting around and letting Penny stew in her curiosity.

"Did you really fight that shark for your teeth?"

"Well, I have Black Finn's chompers, don't I?"

She shot back, "That doesn't mean you fought him."

"With these two hands, aye, and me old belt."

Marmoona's new staff leg took some getting used to. (For him to walk on and for us to bear seeing him suffer. It didn't help that he had to learn the ropes on the berg's icy-slick surface.)

When hunger got the better of us, we knew it was time to venture out of the cavern. After taking the boat back to the mouth of the well, it was clear that escape would test our mettle.

I rowed into the circle o' light streaming from above. The bucket still bobbed softly in the water. Penny pulled in the wet rope. Its drippy end was wildly frayed by Fernobarb's chomp.

"This one can't jump that high," Marmoona stated apologetically.

"None of us be makin' that jump. And even if we stood on each other's shoulders, we'd still be five or six people too short to reach the openin'."

We searched for another way out. Thar were so many different passageways, we were lucky to find one that offered a ray of hope. Most of the caverns had a few small holes in the ceiling. They were all very high, out of reach and, again, too small to be of any use. One corridor, though, had a rather large shaft o' light skimming over the dark surface. The ceiling dipped low here. As the boat drifted closer, Marmoona swung an oar to hit the rock. "This one almost close enough." By eye alone, I could tell Marmoona wasn't going to fit. And if he wouldn't fit, ye could starve me for a whole month 'n' I still wouldn't be able to get through. Before I could utter a word, Penny was on her feet.

"I can fit." Just like that, she volunteered for the job.

"Are ye sure?"

She dumped the long length of rope in the bucket. "I'm sure I don't want to stay down here forever."

I stood with Marmoona on the side ledges of the li'l boat. We leaned in toward each other and locked hands, forming a tall triangle. Penny balanced the bucket on me shoulders, caught her shoe on me belt and pulled herself up to the opening.

"Don't forget the bucket 'n' the rope."

She reached back down, took them from me and began crawling up to the surface. Her legs dangled for a bit while we sat back in the boat.

"I'm going now, all right?"

"Ye be safe, me Lucky Penny."

"This one wants to see you again."

Was it dangerous out thar? Aye, but thar weren't no other way to do it. Most people would be scared to run round up top with Fernobarb on a vicious prowl, but bravery outmatches fear, and I don't know many people with more courage filling thar heart than that li'l girl.

She seemed to have been gone for days, but it was probably a lot closer to a few minutes when we heard her again. "Redbeard! Marmoona!" she whispered. "Which way is the well? I don't remember exactly how to get there."

"This one knows. Make your steps to the flat place and the air that goes pop. Go up and down with the water. Have care, trouble there."

"Do ye have all that?"

"Yes, I think so. Goodbye. I don't want to be too long."

I turned to the speckle-belly. "Marmoona, what are we goin' to do about Fernobarb when we get out o' here?"

"It's the bad one's island. What will that one do with you?"

"I don't care if it's Fernobarb's island. Ye live here too, and ye should live in peace."

"This one waters the island and lives in peace."

"What do ye mean?"

"This one plants and helps the island grow so Fernobarb will let this one live."

"The two of ye have an arrangement, do ye?"

Marmoona nodded.

"But the beast took yer bloody leg!" I cried.

His face was so calm. "But Beardface put it back."

"I replaced yer leg because I'm yer true-blue friend."

Marmoona felt the intricate carvings along his former staff. "And I'll help you get rid of Fernobarb fer the very same reason." I stared long at the speckle-belly's long, gangly leg and then at his wooden stump. "Marmoona, I'm awful sorry I went to the ruins fer water. It looks like the wrong fella paid the price fer me mistake."

It took some effort, but Marmoona finally saw that Fernobarb needed to be done away with. We debated several schemes, many of them disastrous attempts made by the ancient band of humans. Together we put the pieces in place. Our plot involved a life-sized stuffed Captain Redbeard (me!), a hole in the ground, the barbed branches of the sheknee'a-tu-uh tree (just like the stick Marmoona used for his staff) and a lot of help from me hardworking friends, including Gaya Bird. Oh, and, Li'l Whisker, ye'll get a kick out of this: at one point the plot also called for fire to rain down from the sky. But I don't want to spoil it for ye.

Marmoona and I floated quietly in the well. We were both quite relieved when li'l Miss Morun ducked her head down the hole. The bucket jerked up as it reached the end of the line, swaying madly to and fro. "It's all right," Penny called down. "I already tied it to the rope outside."

When we had first come to the well, the bucket sat afloat on the water, with many feet o' line submerged below. Now, after Fernobarb's bite and whatever looping knot Penny used to secure it outside, the bucket hovered just out of arm's reach.

"This one to go first."

"O' course! Indeed!" I boosted Marmoona's good foot in me cupped hands. "Up ye go." His wooden leg slipped along the rope, but he used his toes to inspiring advantage. Why, he made it out of the well in about the same time I was hoping to do it in.

Out around the stump of the well, the warm sun soothed our chilled skin. "This one thinks it a good idea indeed."

Squinting from the glare, Penny responded, "What idea?"

Marmoona smiled. "To do away with the bad one, Fernobarb."

Her face went colorless. "But . . . is that even possible?"

I placed a hand on the young girl's shoulder. "We'll soon answer that question, me Lucky Penny. All in good time."

The hole we needed—and what a beauty she was—was already dug. Marmoona showed us how to make proper shovels from the shells o' the eyeboloney. It was so deep and wide, I'm sure ye could have upended a fruit cart down into the hollow and still have had room to spare. All our work was done in shifts, usually at night with someone on watch, high in the fronds of the zagging palms. While

I worked in the clutches of Gaya Bird to transport the barbed sheknee'a-tu-uk spikes from a cape on the west side o' the island, Penny worked fast and hard on creating the scarecrow version of meself. She used the material from the hammock to fashion some pants, and I had to forfeit an old coat and me onliest hat for the rest. Three dark pieces of spongefruit lashed together became me head, and the twigs she poked in the bottom made a dashing replica o' me infamous beard. And what to stuff it with, ye ask? Jelly beans, o' course! The *Picaroon* was still loaded with 'em. I stopped by the ship to check her progress. "Don't ye think ye've filled the coat a bit much?"

"It looks fine to me, Redbeard. Pillowy, just like you are."

I decided to keep silent.

"Do you really think this is the best idea?"

"Sure as day, Penny. Marmoona will wake Fernobarb. Then Marmoona will run 'n' hide outside the cave. Once in the open, Fenobarb'll see the oversized, jelly-bean-filled likeness o' me and charge like an ill wind. What the beast won't know is that right behind its meal, covered under a layer of zaggin' fronds, a deep pit awaits. And that pit is filled to the brim with hungry spikes. As Fernobarb gets skewered, I'll be circlin' overhead with a fiery spear to cast down into that evil skull. And as the column of smoke dances to the sky, the island will rejoice in its new freedom."

Back at the cape I was gathering the last batch of spikes. Around the pit, Penny and Marmoona worked to plant the spiked branches in the soil of the pit. "Marmoona, what about the spitflower poison? It kills the black jumpers. If we poured a whole pitcher of it on Fernobarb while the beast slept, wouldn't that kill it, too?"

The speckle-belly leaned against the side of a spike to ponder the question. "This one thinks not."

"But you don't know for sure."

"No."

"I have a whole pitcher in my hut-bush—"

He stopped her before she could go on. "That one not a good idea," he warned.

Penny left to find a bigger pounding stone. Marmoona was busy preparing the pit and didn't realize until he'd finished that the girl had been gone so long. He walked through the woods, calling here and thar, "This one is looking for you!" When he had no luck in the jungle, he tried her hut-bush. But still no Penny. Marmoona fell into worry and limped-ran to the very last place she should have been.

High in an alcove overlooking Fernobarb's lair, he found Penny nervously prepared to make her move. She managed to lug a huge wooden pot of the spitflower poison up into the crevasse. She grasped the pot's lip and tipped it over the edge. The container was so full, its weight forced it to topple over. Poison splashed down, showering stickily over the instantly enraged beast.

"This one is coming!" Marmoona screamed, and grabbed Penny's hand.

The pot 'n' poison slipped far below into the lair, but Lucky Penny was safe. A roar was unleashed and Marmoona scurried outside, moving as best he could on the new leg. This I was able to see from above. Unfortunately, I also saw that the pit wasn't ready. "Why did they start the trap too early?" I yelled up to Gaya Bird.

Marmoona hobbled along and vanished for a bit beneath the cover of trees. Fernobarb tore after him down the path. Rain pelted the island with a vengeance.

The beast lunged at scarecrow Redbeard, knocking the hat far into the shrubbery. I couldn't stand the sight of those beans, much less the thought of throwing 'em into me belly again. The vile creature wolfed me down as it collapsed into the pit. The few standing spikes pierced its skin. Marmoona hobbled away, slowly heading toward Twin Star Peak.

From the spiked pit, Fernobarb let loose another unsettling cry, and, as if to extinguish the sound, a lightning bolt shattered the sky in search of its source. The air between us and the failed trap blurred into the streaked grays of a storm. Without hesitation, the great bird banked to the right. She made a tight enough turn to lead us back in the direction of the crystal peak. A few quick flaps over the wind had us picking up speed, and it was a good thing too, for right on our heels a wicked howl of a wind gave chase. Columns of sparking electricity erupted all around, forcing the bird to weave between them. We came so close to some of the bolts, I could feel the heat in the brass buttons o' me shirt.

Far down in the overgrowth, Marmoona scrambled. In a fit he let out sputtering pants with every hop and hurdle over the island's many obstacles. This was a creature in terror. Thar was no doubt about the fear that was making him flee. I spotted Lucky Penny hiding in a hollow, watching it all unfold. Scanning the beach, I found a long, dark thundercloud steadily winding its way up to Fundorado's peak. Fernobarb's deep groan announced the arrival of its snaking storm, slowly trailing behind the frightful beast.

Li'l Whisker, the expression on that old Marmoona's face was enough to break a pirate's heart. He knew the beast was after him, and he knew he was done for if he couldn't make a proper escape. Me speckle-bellied friend came to one of the large rock clusters at the base of Twin Star Peak, where he stretched to pull himself up and move on to the next one.

A black howl ripped from Fernobarb, and half a moment later another bolt of lightning fell from the clouds that followed. The sky sizzled in the air where we hung. Almost wobbling along, the terrible Fernobarb was most certainly slower than the speedy predator I had witnessed at the lava lake. Of course, that was before it wolfed down the jelly-bean-stuffed scarecrow. Li'l Whisker, I never did think I would see the day when those jelly beans would prove to be a good thing.

Sad as sad can be, that poor Marmoona tripped and found himself sitting right up in the darkest part of the beast's shadow. Thar it was, hunched up into one muscle with eyes that had shrunk to the size of a peephole and a pipe-organ wheeze that dampened the draft with fright. Every breath the evil thing took was a struggle.

Slowly Marmoona sank against the rock and stared blankly at the vicious face above him. The beast's belly gurgled and a thick paw fired up and hammered down at the cowering Marmoona. Chips of stone flew with the scrape of the angry claws. From the safe distance of a well-timed jump, Marmoona stared at the four white scars that now ran along the very spot where he had sat seconds before.

On the boulders the beast stood. The speckle-bellied Marmoona moved ever so slowly back toward the monster. Even the slightest of movements attracted the beast's attention. It half grunted through its fat nose, and its powerful shoulders twitched in anticipation of an order to move. Cautiously Marmoona crept closer. The beast's body jerked, its feet never leaving the rocks, and the yellow critter flung himself back in terror. But soon it became clear that the monster had its sights set elsewhere. In the distance it spotted Penny trying to escape up another path to the peak, and the vile creature began its ascent after her.

I watched in bewilderment as Gaya Bird and I circled overhead. Above the mountain thar wasn't much I could rightly do for the brave girl, except feel a strange kind o' blue, knowing I had somehow gotten her into this mess.

Not too far from the waterfall cave entrance, the evil thing peered down at the fury below. On its hind legs the beast stood, voicing its rage in a rabid roar. The gray clouds answered the sound with a chorus of thunder. Lightning cracked down; one bolt buried itself in the giant bird's left wing. The lightning must have weighed a ton, as it sent Gaya Bird straight to the ground at a terrifying rate. We crashed to the dirt near the peak. A fall from the sky doesn't feel too good, especially if yer the landing pad for an abnormally heavy bird. I knew the spot well, for it was a stone's throw from me treasure chest's hiding spot. If it hadn't been for that tangle we had in the ruins, I would've already had me trunk safely hidden away in the cave.

Beneath the bird I lay, fighting for a breath against the weight upon me back. The good news is that I wasn't hurt too badly. The bad news is that I was trapped. A dull whine spilled from Gaya Bird's beak. She was hurt and didn't seem like she could move. Me head just barely peeked out from the ruff of feathers, and I saw the beast working its way up the slope. Thar was clumsiness in its movement, its pace slowed by the stomach-churning candies. The space between us gradually shrank until Fernobarb was upon us. The injured bird lay motionless at the feet of the livid creature. Rumbles shot off in the sky. The evil creature raised its body in the air and dove at the bird. Under the thick wing I hid me head. Me heart trembled, but the ravaging I prepared meself for never came.

In the dark I waited for a spell, listening for any clue to what was going on outside. I forced me face out from the bird's protective hold and scoured the ground for a trace of the wicked beast. It was nowhere to be seen, but with me head popped out I could hear the creature's massive body struggling up the craggy path farther up the mountain.

"Fernobarb! Up here!" Penny shouted.

I heard the sound of rocks striking rock. To slip out

from under the wing, I hugged the dirt and scooted little by little past the feathery cover. First me left boot was free, and I pushed even harder to get me entire leg out. More plaintive whispers came from the bird, so I was careful not to move in a way that would add to her pain. As I pulled me arm back from the bird, the last of me trapped body was freed.

Straight up the mountain, the beast closed in on its prey. Penny flailed one arm and hurled a stone at it. Just above the mouth of the cave, the speckle-belly rested. Behind the ledge where he stood, the rushing waterfall split in two, spilling to either side of the mountain's gaping entrance. He looked spent. His legs were gathered under him in a kneeling slouch; his spindly fingers gently touched his wounded wooden leg.

Making her way over to Marmoona, the girl still taunted the beast. "Come get me, you monster! I'm not afraid!"

The brave young lady crouched and hoisted a helmet-sized stone with her trembling arms. "Time for careful, Penny Girl!" Both Marmoona and I watched in astonishment as she swung the rock back 'n' forth like the pendulum of a grandfather clock. She released the small boulder from her high position, and it flew a bit before ricocheting off the hard mountainside. The stone collected speed as it shot downhill. It launched off a ledge, smashing the beast's left horn right from his skull. (Though she still claims it was her intention all along, I like to remind her that she earned the name Lucky Penny fair 'n' square.)

Thar was no thought behind Fernobarb's steps that brought it to the large span of stone that spread out from the cave opening, and, oddly enough, those same steps carried even less sound. Penny was stoic in the shadow of the predator's advance. If Fernobarb's eyes had a color, I think it was here that I saw it. They grew just enough to study brave li'l Penny before falling back to their peephole size. The beast's green eyes were now pressed far into his skull.

Without thinking, I put me feet to full sail across the short distance that stretched up to the cave where the trunk was stashed. As the beast was about to break into a leap, its tail floundered upon the ground, its legs pulsed and it arched through the air. The two front feet met the rock with a clap. This jump made by the evil creature brought it just a jaw's snap from Penny.

"Jump, Penny! Jump!"

Penny leapt like a lizard and clawed her way up the waterfalls' rock divide. The beast fumbled as the expert climber vanished from its clutches. Diving after her, Fernobarb landed deep within the mouth of the cave.

I hoisted me treasure to me shoulder and charged after Fernobarb. A glow lit Marmoona's face. He saw what I saw. This was our chance to free Fundorado Island. I hurled me trunk within the mouth of the cave.

With chest and hands I pushed the trunk as far as it

would go. Marmoona and I beat ourselves against it, shoving the wicked devil into the mountain's darkness. A sharp squeak stuttered between the wood and rock, making sure it sealed the entrance. Lucky for me, the cave

Thou Shalt Not Debung

hadn't worked out so well as a hiding spot, seeing how the trunk couldn't rightly fit all the way in the entrance. With the cork in place, Fernobarb was imprisoned. I heard the monster try to smash through, but its efforts only caused a single, distant, muffled thud. The treasure wasn't going anywhere and neither was the beast. Here they would sit forevermore.

We headed down the slope, Marmoona and I, to take care of Gaya Bird as she calmly stirred. From a nearby tree, I pulled some sticky fruit to feed her, and the Marmoona plucked the blackened feathers from her wing. From that height on the mountain we could see Fernobarb's storm drying out around the island. The clouds peeled away so the purty sun could warm us up. I sat thar, tucked safely 'tween Gaya Bird and Marmoona, each of us trying to catch our breath. Just then we heard a few faint hiccups coming from atop the cave's corked entrance. I hustled over to help Penny down. She lowered her tiny fingers and I swallowed them up in me husky palm. We both closed our eyes (well, I closed mine, and I reckon she did likewise), and somehow we found the might to get her down safe and sound. With her in me arms, I made me way back to Marmoona and Gaya. Thar the li'l lass rested, against me chest.

Before fading off, Lucky Penny looked into me eyes. "Now you can never leave Fundorado Island."

"How do ye mean, me li'l one?"

"Look at your treasure. It's stuck."

"Right ye are, Penny. Wherever me treasure lies, so rests me heart."

And so, Matey, that be the long and short of me true-life adventure. And if yer to know the truth, I must tell ye that thar wouldn't be a single word of it written down if it wasn't for Penny. She told me it wouldn't be an adventure if I didn't share it and put it in writing. I told her I never did too good using the proper words and such and she promised she'd do her best to help me. And so she has. Thar were plenty of moments that might have downright slipped from me feeble memory if it wasn't for Penny being thar to remind me. It took us quite a while to get the whole story down for ye. How long exactly, I can't rightly say, for here on Fundorado time doesn't work the way it does at sea. The days and nights float by with the sweet rhythm of the ocean waves, and thar be no reason for us to keep track o' them 'cause we know they'll be thar forever. No need for an old-fashioned calendar carved into a tree. No need for a calendar at all. We spend every unmarked second enjoying all the island has to offer. So much still to be discovered—Li'l Whisker, ye can't imagine!

Redbeard's Den has proven to be a fine home. Gaya Bird was good enough to build a new nest at the entrance to me hovel. That way she can sleep right thar next to me at night, barring the door and keeping me own sleep-walking body from getting into trouble. The *Picaroon,* no longer seaworthy, has taken up a satisfactory use as Marmoona's new haunt. (I hope ye didn't think I wouldn't replace the home I ravaged upon me arrival.)

The treasure I so dearly loved will never be more valuable than it is now—wedged in the rock, locking that dreadful beast and his clouded powers deep underground. It'll stay thar forever. For if some greedy fortune hunter was able to remove it, he would find that the riches come at the unfortunate price of an enraged Fernobarb. Far below the surface the beast remains, scaring up enough force to stir the island's bedrock into a storm and loosen it from the earth. Like a captainless ship, the island drifts about the seven seas. Thar is no destination. We wander wherever the beast takes us. Of course, the island's shifting isn't that bad, save for one truly tragic puzzler: if Fundorado is endlessly moving, it'll be right near impossible for anyone to find it. As sure as north hates south, the thought of not being able to share the island's wonders makes me blue.

Oh, Li'l Whisker, with every shooting star that streaks across the night, I wish for the chance to give ye me own personal tour of the island and let ye experience the wonderment of Fundorado. For now, all I can do is tuck me story into Gaya Bird's beak and hope she can find a way to get it to ye. Me friend, ye have me word, this isn't the last ye've heard of Fundorado Island. New adventures spring up under me boots every day. I'll keep a weather eye open for Gaya Bird's return and hope that, by some stroke of sparkletricity, I'll hear from ye soon. And maybe one day we'll even meet, Li'l Whisker . . . just maybe.

Yer true friend,
Captain Redbeard
With help from Lucky Penny

AN AFTERWORD
by
Maxwell Dormpier III
Executive Publisher

Mr. Sherwood insisted that the great Gaya Bird will one day return. To that end, he has vowed to remain aboard his vessel day and night, with his letter in hand, looking for the silver-backed bird over the horizon. He has made the rather kind offer to deliver any and all letters Mr. Redbeard's readers might wish to send.

I have included my address below. If you would like to send any messages to my attention, I will be happy to forward them to Mr. Sherwood. He will ensure that every last one finds its way into the giant beak of Gaya Bird . . . and onto the adventure-riddled shores of Fundorado.

Captain Redbeard
c/o Random House Children's Books
1745 Broadway, Mail Drop 9-2
New York, NY 10019

Redbeard's Guide to the Strange and Unfamiliar (for Yer Average Landlubber)

AVAST: A command that means stop, as in, "Avast thar, that tickles."

AYE: A quick and easy way to say yes.

BILGE: The bottommost part of a ship's hull. Best things to store down thar are darkness, stink and the bulk of a ship's loose vermin.

BLACK FINN: Only the most frightening shark in Flotsom Bay (if not the world). Naturally, I mopped the ocean floor with him. (Boy, were those bottom-feeders ever upset.)

BOW: All the way thar at the very front of the ship. (Be looking for the figurehead, which adorns the bow.)

BUCCANEER: An adventurer wanting to make certain that any particular outing bodes well for the purse.

CHANTY: This here be a song sang solely by pirates entirely for the enjoyment of thar fella pirates, mostly late at night. (I don't too much fancy the early-morning chanties.)

COMPANIONWAY: Whether it's up or down ye wish to go, ye'll do neither without these shipshape stairs to get ye thar.

CONCERTINA: A sweet-sounding instrument of the accordion family. (Jimmy's being me own personal favorite.)

CROW'S NEST: A lookout spot at the top of the mast. Legend has it that if ye find an actual crow (not a pelican!) making a nest in the crow's nest, yer ship is doomed to sink in three months' time.

DAVEY JONES'S LOCKER: Only one way of putting this: the very bottommost part of the ocean. The key here being that once ye go thar, ye usually don't return.

DINGHY: A very small boat with a very silly name.

FERNOBARB: Plain and simple, this here be the face of evil. What else can ye call the beast who tries to keep the paradise of Fundorado Island all to its lonesome self?

FIGUREHEAD: The figure carved on the front (bow) of a ship. Some crews make up stories to tell about thar figurehead, and a certain nearsighted crew member of the *Picaroon* (Monkey Fist) had a crush on our mermaid figurehead for the better part of a week.

FUNDORADO ISLAND: A magical piece of land— Wait a blasted minute! For the proper and full definition see: *Fundorado Island: Redbeard's Discoveries (And His Adventures Too) by Yers Truly, Captain Redbeard (With Help from a Lucky Penny)*. If ye can't find a good enough definition in thar, something's wrong.

GALLEON: Usually a nice big ship with a squarelike shape to it, particularly fancied by the Spaniards for shipping goods across the seas.

GANGPLANK: A portable bridge used to get on 'n' off a ship. If ye be a naughty crew member, ye don't want to be near one.

GREAT-GRANDPA GUST: A mighty wind with magical timing. When this current o' air sweeps up around ye, it usually delivers ye from a pickle. But be ye warned: the price ye pay is being magically changed into whatever it is ye hate the most.

HULL: The true sailor's way of referring to the main frame 'n' body of a ship. Ye might call it the skin of any seagoing vessel.

JOLLY ROGER: The pirate flag of the skull and crossbones. It's supposed to strike fear in the hearts of those who see it, but skeletons can't do too much harm. They just sit thar forever with that foolish grin always plastered to thar face.

LANDLUBBER: One who's more fond of land than the ocean. The sort that gets seasick from listening to the tides in a seashell.

LI'L WHISKER: I'm hopin' ye aren't too confused with this one, since it's me own personal way of addressing ye as I tell ye me story.

MADAGASCAR: An island ruled by the fiercest o' pirates. If yer on Madagascar, no matter where ye live, yer as far away from home as ye can be.

MARMOONA: Sometimes I call him Speckle-Belly, but his true name is Marmoona. He's a true friend indeed, too, willing to share his vast island knowledge with curious newcomers. The wild thing roster wouldn't be complete without him.

MAST: A tall pole used for supporting the sails 'n' rigging.

ONOMATOPOEIA: Actually, I don't know the meaning of this word, but I heard it once and it's been driving me crazy ever since. So ye best look it up on yer own and I'll leave a space for the proper definition.

____

____

PICAROON: The sweet ship of yers truly, Captain Redbeard, known and respected and feared by all sailors throughout the seven seas. Received as a gift from the good people of Crook Haven.

PORT: The word to use when yer talking about the left. Not too often that the whole crew's facing the same direction at the same time. So whenever ye hear "port" yer meant to pretend yer facing toward the bow (whether ye really are or not don't matter) and from that point ye look left.

PUMPERNICKEL: Quite a good bread indeed. It's brown and tasty, a perfect combination.

RATIONS: Food on a ship. Sometimes it's bad; sometimes it's worse.

RIGGING: The ropes and all that keep the sails standing right in the wind's way. I once sailed with a pirate named Franky the Flying Fish. He ran away from the circus to become a pirate and would do his trapeze act in the rigging, much to the joy o' the crew.

ROGUE: Any fella or gal who goes against the grain. They ain't too keen on rules and the like.

SALMAGUNDI: A stew with everything in it—everything, that is, save for flavor.

SCURVY ROCK: Thar be no definition found here. Just a friendly reminder ye best keep yer promise.

SCUTTLEBUTT: No-good rumors 'n' flights of fancy. If it sounds too good to be true it probably is—except for Fundorado Island, o' course.

SHIPSHAPE: If ye be on a ship, ye want it to be shipshape. It means everything is set, and smooth sailing is to be had. If yer boat ain't shipshape, ye'll know in good time, when ye have to start swimming.

SIROCCO: A hot wind famed for its speed.

SPARKLETRICITY: I'm afraid this word can't be summed up, Li'l Whisker. Closest ye can say is that it's Fundorado's magical power, which pulls ye in and guides ye to the island. Can't be found anywhere else but this here paradise.

STARBOARD: Same situation as with port applies here, only now it means to the right.

STERN: The very back of the ship.

STOWAWAY: Any variation of landlubber, swab or generally misguided soul tucked away on a ship where no one can see him.

STOVE-AWAY: Same thing as a stowaway, only a different word for it when applied to Lucky Penny.

SWAB: To wash the deck with water, usually dirtier than the very deck itself, or the poor chap tied to this duty.

TEMPEST TANTRUM: A trademark of Fernobarb. When he's at his worst and he uses all his meanness to kick up the shores of Fundorado Island into an unnatural storm.

For those of you interested in elements of the captain's log that were not published, you are in luck. Rufus Sherwood has assembled his very own space on the Web to display the many pages missing from the book you now hold. Hear Rufus tell in his own words how the tale was delivered to him, read accounts of the historical Redbeard and ponder the wrinkled maps available nowhere else. When more develops on the Fundorado Island front, Mr. Sherwood's site will fill you in.

www.RedbeardsIsland.com